LOOK PAST

LOOK PAST

Eric Devine

RP|TEENS
PHILADELPHIA • LONDON

For those who see
beyond the surface
to what lies within

Books published by Running Press are available at
special discounts for bulk purchases in the United States
by corporations, institutions, and other organizations. For
more information, please contact the Special Markets
Department at the Perseus Books Group, 2300 Chestnut
Street, Suite 200, Philadelphia, PA 19103, or call
(800) 810-4145, ext. 5000, or e-mail
special.markets@perseusbooks.com.

ISBN 978-0-7624-5921-6

Library of Congress Control Number: 2016940452

E-book ISBN 978-0-7624-6122-6

9   8   7   6   5   4   3   2   1

Digit on the right indicates the number of this printing

Front cover image: Face © Thinkstock Images/123FirstLine

Designed by T.L. Bonaddio
Edited by Lisa Cheng and Andrea Cascardi
Typography: Fairfield and Frank Reaction

Published by Running Press Teens,
An Imprint of Perseus Books, a Division of PBG Publishing, LLC,
A Subsidiary of Hachette Book Group, Inc.

Running Press Book Publishers
2300 Chestnut Street
Philadelphia, PA 19103-4371

Visit us on the web!
www.runningpress.com/rpkids

Searching is not the same as finding. Right now I don't want to do either. But right now isn't about me. It's about this crowd of most of the entire town, huddled beneath the pines, listening to my uncle Tom. It's about the instructions he's giving about how we're going to look, and how we're hopefully going to find. It's about the who we're trying to find. Or, depending on how you look at it, the what. It's about Mary.

"So once we're in the woods, stay as close as possible. Move as a line, and go *slow*. I can't overstate that. Move like you're looking for your car keys. If you find anything out here that seems like it doesn't belong, or that might be Mary's, you blow that whistle around your neck." Tom looks us over and he catches my eye, holds it for a long moment, and then nods to the group.

We turn, take our places, and start walking.

It's been a week since the Amber Alert went out, since the town began worrying for their "daughter," and then as the days passed, started wondering if a killer's on the loose. No one has slept or eaten or prayed without thinking of her. No one with a heart.

It's been seven days since Mary fought with her boyfriend, Calder. Seven days and one hour since she fought with her dad, Reverend Matthison.

Now, I walk with my friend Charlie and my girlfriend, Beth, with Calder and Mary's father side by side amid the reverend's congregation, who are all holding hands. I've got my eye on Calder and Reverend Matthison. *We* do. The entire town does. Religious or not, they were the last to see her alive, and everyone knows that statistic.

"Hey, Avery, you all right?" Charlie asks, bringing my attention back to center, to the ground before me.

"No." It's all I can say, because what I'm thinking, what I'm imagining, are too much. If I said them, my uncle would have to lock me up for questioning just to appease everyone within earshot. Fortunately, Charlie nods, scratches his beard, and moves on.

Beth puts her hand in mine, squeezes tight. I squeeze back.

We keep walking, heads down, wordless, and soon step over a dead, moss-covered tree. It's rained for a week straight, and we sink into the mud on the other side.

Charlie and Beth get free quickly, but my right foot is covered. "Give me a hand."

They both offer one and pull me loose. My foot makes a sucking fart sound. Charlie smiles. I try not to, but fail. "Did you shit your pants, Av?" he asks.

I laugh and check my pants as a joke. "Nope, looks good."

Beth laughs, too, but then to our left we hear deep male voices. "Quit messing around, Chase. We all know it's just a shit show down there."

"You wearing a fake dick today?" one of them says to me.

The jokes sting, but I refuse to look at these assholes. It's what they want, and I'm long past giving anyone here what they want.

Charlie doesn't mind speaking up. "We're all here for one thing, right? Let's just do that." His voice is a growl.

"Your point?" another one of them asks.

Beth steps to them, her red hair snapping along her back as she does. "Really? You need it explained more?"

One of them says, "Whatever. Move on, you fucking freaks."

I bite my lip and close my eyes, wishing them away. But we move on.

When we're far enough away from them, Charlie whispers "Sorry."

"Not your fault," I say.

We step over wet leaves and patches of mud and heaps of pine needles. The only noise is the sound of cracking twigs and the occasional low voices. It's maddening, all this plodding and silence. No one's blowing a whistle or yelling about having found anything. Part of me hopes it stays this way, but the rest feels like an overwhelming truth: Mary's out here. We wouldn't be searching the woods if we were just looking for evidence of where she might have run away to.

The silence continues until we come to a bend of the stream that runs through these woods. One I know too well. I stop and I listen to the present and to the past.

Third grade is when I realized I wasn't like the other girls. It was more than not wanting to play with their toys and hop in on their games of dress-up or playing "mommy" or gossiping. I felt a distance between us. An absolute difference in who they were and who I was. Nothing I had the ability to articulate, except in my drawings. In them I dressed myself like Dad, in a shirt and tie. Mary loved those drawings.

But she didn't love them when the other boys drew themselves that way. I think once they saw the cute, ponytailed girl giving me attention they copied me in hope of similar affection. It didn't work that way. Mary liked that I, who looked like a girl, with my hair still long, drew myself as a boy. "Why?" she asked.

"Because that's who I am," I said.

"What do you mean?" She pressed into me, getting a closer look at my drawing. I loved that contact, relished how her face lit up at my answer.

"I'm me."

And from then we were friends, not inseparable, but close. She kept to skirts and dresses while I cut my hair and wore jeans. I watched her while I played tag and capture the flag. She laughed and played her part in the girl drama of who liked whom and who was popular and who wasn't, but always with an eye out for me. And when I'd go to her house, there was an effortless way about her that I couldn't understand. So one day I asked, "Why are you different with me?"

"You mean than with the other girls?"

Her saying it that way didn't even sting. Maybe that's because I was still wondering who I was, or maybe it's just because Mary had said it. Either way, I said, "No. You're different with me than you are with anyone else. You don't mind when I don't want to play princesses. You let me be the dad when we play house." I paused here. I remember how nervous I felt about what I was going to say, even though I knew Mary was fine with it. "You don't laugh at me when I say I'm a boy. Why?"

She smiled and her cheeks tucked up around her eyes. "That's because there's no one else like you, Avery."

And if there was any question as to whether I loved her it was obliterated by her smile, that answer.

But in eighth grade there was an intensity in Mary that I'd never seen before. She felt it, too; I could tell. The way I'd catch her looking at me told me so. She was seeing me with my short hair and my budding breasts flattened into nonexistence by my binder, and liking what she saw. Mary was looking at me in the way Beth looks at me now.

She was still willing to spend some of her summer with me, the times when her father was busy with work. Because if he so much as saw me coming up the driveway, I'd be banished from the house. So when he was busy with his flock, we'd hang out like we always had, cutting through the woods or keeping to the shadows of her property to stay cool, because I wouldn't swim. Not until that day. And only because she asked.

"Come on, Avery. No one's home. Mom's out with my aunt, and Dad's working on his sermon." Mary sat on her bed and leaned forward with her pleading eyes.

Everything in me screamed no, but I said, "Okay."

She bounced up and clapped. "Yay! It's just *so* hot today. I need to get in the water."

She went to her drawer and pulled out a bikini.

Mary saw the look on my face when she turned. "Oh, right. You don't have a suit." And she doesn't have a brother. Yet, she held up a finger and scampered out of the room. I expected her to come back with one of her dad's bathing suits, which would have been three times my size, but she held up a pair of board shorts.

"Are those Calder's?" I asked, a little surprised, a little jealous. How could I not be? He had the official status of *boyfriend*.

She blushed. "Yeah. He left them last week."

I turned away because I didn't like how seeing her so excited made me feel so dispensable. "How long have you been together?"

"Three months, two days." She giggled and I shook my head. I couldn't be angry with her for being happy. But I could be frustrated that I wasn't the one she was happy over.

"All right. Grab me a towel. I'll change in the bathroom."

Mary's bathroom, fortunately, has only a small mirror, which I easily avoided. I wriggled out of my binder, immediately pulling my T-shirt back on. Calder's shorts were a little loose, but they felt awesome on me, like I'd stepped into his skin for a moment.

And maybe that's why things happened as they did, because I felt right, inside out, which has been a rarity my entire life. Or maybe it had nothing to do with Calder's shorts and everything to do with Mary: how beautiful she looked in her bikini, her hair pulled back and eyes so open, taking me in. Or maybe it was her gentle way. Mary hopped into the swimming hole down the hill from her house, the one fed by the stream, and then coaxed me in. She had to, because I wanted to run away, back to the house and change and to stop feeling what I was feeling. I was overwhelmed in that moment, so much that the cold water did nothing to dampen the surging inside.

I dipped underwater to try and calm down, but when I came up, nothing had changed. Mary was staring at me with more desire than she ever had before. I don't know what it was about that moment or how I looked to her, but it changed everything between us.

I didn't stop her from moving away from the edge and swimming across to me. I watched her approach and I pleaded with my eyes, and she understood.

Mary kissed me. My first. And there are times when life sucks and no one sees me and I remember this moment, the first time a girl accepted who I am. Mary pulled me close and held nothing back. And I was hers, forever, even though I knew that could never happen.

◈

Staring at the water rushing by, swollen with the rain, I am overwhelmed again. I move to the base of a tree and sit. The ground is wet and I will look like I shit myself, but it doesn't matter. Mary's gone. Some monster in this town got her. I feel it like I felt that moment, startling me awake.

"Charlie?"

"Yeah?"

"Who do you think it is?"

He squats down next to me. "What do you mean?"

I scowl. "Don't pull that. You know what I mean." Charlie and I became friends because of our interest in forensics. We've stayed friends because he's as understanding as my father.

He sighs and looks deeper into the woods. "You know you shouldn't think like that. She could have just run away."

Beth clears her throat. "Listen to him. It makes sense. I mean, everyone loves her. She has no enemies."

"That's not true," I say.

"What isn't?" Beth asks.

"Everyone has enemies."

Charlie shifts his position. "Name one."

I have only one for Mary, but he's too close, and I

don't know if the memory has been distorted because of all that has happened, whether I'm remembering correctly, or if I've unearthed only pieces and have left too much buried. But if I'm right, then he's here, searching, and aware of whether or not we're in the right place.

❖

I pull into my driveway, cold and wet and sore. I dig into my car's console and pull out my pack of mini cigars and lighter. The flame feels good in my cold hands and the smoke smells sweet. Both are welcome, because my body is numb and I am sick of the smell of mud and woods. It wasn't as bad as last week when we slogged through the rain, searching. Then it was one useless excursion after the next, just like Tom said it would be. The rain poured so hard, visibility was for shit. Today, Tom called off the search party because it was getting too dark. At least we made it that long. But he also called it because we found nothing. Just like before. Not a trace of anything. That rain. One week of it could wash away anything.

I take a last puff of my cigar and flick it out the window, except it bounces back and falls into my lap. I pick it up and stare at the ember, feel the heat of it close to my nose. I say, "I'm sorry, Mary," and hear the high-pitched break, not the rasp I'm working on. I want to jam the ember in my eye to keep the tears back.

I rein them in and head inside.

Whatever Dad's cooking makes my stomach growl. I haven't eaten since breakfast, so I am compelled to open the oven. The heat and the aroma are heavenly.

"Hey, Av." Dad stands up from his computer in the office nook across the room and makes his way toward me. "I am so sorry, buddy. Tom called me a little while ago. Told me it was a bust." He wraps me up and squeezes so tight. I relax into his embrace.

After a moment I pull away. "It was. But we covered a lot of ground. We'll cover more tomorrow."

"That's good. Tom okay?"

He still worries about his brother like I do Tyler. I like that Dad checks up on Officer Chase.

"I think so. I'm sure he's exhausted."

"He's been exhausted for years." Dad claps me on the shoulder. "Go shower, you reek of"—he sniffs—"vanilla?"

"Yeah." I look at the floor.

"Exactly. You're detracting from the aroma of my fine creation."

I point at the oven. "Pot roast?"

"Yes! With this awesome seasoning from the farmers' market."

"All right. How long?"

Dad checks his watch and guesses a half hour. Mom's schedule eludes us all. I grab a banana from the basket on the counter to tide me over and head back down the front hall toward my room. The door opens and Tyler bounds in.

"Av. Hey. Mom's not home yet, is she?" He looks panicked.

"No, you're good."

He smiles at not being late for dinner, and then his face twists into a frown. "Shit, Av. I heard. Nothing? How could, like, the whole town be out there and find nothing?"

There are a lot of ways, but I keep them to myself. "Yeah. Nothing. But, hey, don't swear. You got another year before high school."

He shakes his head and sniffs like Dad. "And you got another year until you're eighteen. You know, a real adult who can say shit like that."

"Good point." I rub his head and make my way to the bathroom. My clothes feel as if I've already showered in them, and I'm glad to peel them off my body. But my binder's damp and that sucks because this is my favorite. I'll have to settle for another while this dries.

I step in the shower and turn my back to the nozzle, waiting for the heat to untie the knots in my back. All the walking, all the memories, all the things I tried not to think have stitched me up inside out. And my body refuses to loosen. Because it knows. It always knows before I do. It always wants me on guard. For good reason.

But I try to give in to the pull and sit in the tub, letting the water cascade all around. I'm wrong about Mary. She's out there, safe. She's run away. Maybe she's hiding out somewhere until she's made her point. My lower back loosens, and I stretch out over my knees. My breasts brush my legs, but I ignore them. I have to.

Mary's smart enough to have pulled it off. Maybe the fights with her dad and with Calder were on purpose. Maybe she was trying to throw all of us off her tracks. Maybe Calder knows the truth and is playing along. My shoulders slump, and I can practically kiss my shins.

Or not. Word is he wanted sex; she didn't. Or, depending who you listen to, they already had and she didn't want to do it anymore. Either way, she told her dad, thinking he'd help. She couldn't have been more wrong. Ran from her house, screaming. He hurled insults from the door, and that's the last time she's been seen.

The heat of the water has thawed me out, and my brain's working again. I don't have to keep imagining Mary in a shallow grave, or worse, discarded under a tree or in a ravine. Because when I was searching in the woods, that's all I saw wherever I looked. Her. Dead. Demanding answers.

I ease up to my feet and wash my hair and scrub the rest of me, all the parts that I could live with, and those I could certainly live without.

I rinse and towel off, and as I head to my room, hear my mother's voice downstairs. I dress quickly and go with a sports bra and really loose T-shirt.

Mom stands at the bottom of the stairs. I don't understand why she's standing there, coat on, high heels still strapped to her feet. She doesn't have her severe work face. She's not checking her phone. When she looks up, I feel like a child, because whatever it is, her face screams that she wants to protect me from it.

Uncle Tom comes down the hall from the kitchen as I hit the bottom stair. Dad's behind him and his eyes are filled.

I sit. And I shake. And I know.

Tom sits next to me. He looks down, between his knees, and then up and over. "There was this hunter with us today, knows that section of woods well."

Each word paints a picture I don't want to see.

"He, uh, he kind of deviated from the course because he had this feeling. Knew about this old access road."

I want him to stop. I want to scream and to find this hunter and kick him in the balls for what he's made real. But I sit, silent, and wait.

Tom swallows. "He was right, Av. Found Mary's body. She's dead."

I stare into my palm, open and close the fingers around it, but the shaking does not stop. "You're sure?"

The answer doesn't come immediately. Tom doesn't say, "Yes," right away. There's a pause, however brief, before he says, "It has to be."

Mom asks something and possibly Dad, too, but their words are muted, background noise to what I see. Tom's eyes are everywhere at once. The black stubble on his face is almost as dark as what I see in his eyes. Something brutal has happened. Tom is reeling from the evidence. He's trying to get it to filter, to make sense, and is failing.

I look back down and into my palm. I know all there is to know about hiding and about being evasive. Tom is playing my game. He is not my uncle right now. He's Officer Chase, delivering official news that even he does not understand. But I do.

"It wasn't an accident, was it?"

He shifts, uneasy. "I'm not really sure what's what."

"That's not what I asked," I say.

"She's dead, Avery. That's enough for now." He tries to stand, but I grab his wrist and pull him back down.

"No, it's not. Tell me how." My brain is charging through all the chapters I've read, all the websites, all the online chat groups, all the assignments for forensics. There are a million things that can be done to a body. I only want to know one.

But more than that, more than any forensic specifics, I need to know *why* this has happened to Mary. Because that moment almost four years ago solidified my truth. Who I am is not what they believe. Mary was the first to understand this.

Tom stares, his jaw set. And then he softens for an instant. "Someone killed her, Avery." He stands and then the door opens and he goes through it, Dad with him.

The shaking that may have stopped, or that I may have only ignored, jars through me, reenergized. I try to stand, but can't. Mom comes to me, but I don't hear what she says. I feel the rough touch of the carpet against my cheek as I lie on the stairs.

I envision Mary out there in the cold and rain, just like I did today. But now there's no censor, no need to tell myself I'm wrong. Because all that I saw is true. Mary's naked eyes, wide and unseeing, rain pelting her skin, and all the parts of her that I loved. All of her, which someone decided could be discarded.

The shaking turns into a shudder, and my tears finally fall. And I hate every last one, because they don't fall hard enough.

CHAPTER 2

I stare out the window, coffee mug to my lips, but I don't drink and I don't see what's in front of me. One word stretches across the horizon. It is the hills and the sun and the sky: MURDER.

"Avery?"

Mom's voice startles me and I spill coffee down my shirt.

"Sorry, honey. I didn't mean to scare you," she says, reaching for a paper towel.

I take it from her, scowling. I don't like *honey*.

"You don't have to go today. I'll write you a note." She hands over the towel.

I dab, but it achieves next to nothing. "I know. But I don't want to sit home alone."

"Dad will be here," she says.

"Working. Thanks, but it's fine. Really." I smile in spite of myself. I'm so numb I'd smile if a gun were pointed at my head.

"All right, but if you change your mind, call. We'll take care of it." She squeezes me and I pull tighter into her embrace. She holds me until I tell her it's okay and that she should go. I need her to, or else I'd stand here all day.

And as much as it sucks that school is my only option, I do need to get out. I spent yesterday on the couch with my family and Beth and Charlie. Beth held my hand while we cried. Charlie got us drinks so he could leave the room and cry without us seeing it. I don't know why he tried to hide it. Tyler and I didn't bother to.

We watched the news, which was exploitatively awful. It was all this insane coverage of our little town, depicted as the dark epicenter of a murder mystery. Yes, it currently is, but we're more than that. But the reporters don't care about our quaint, tree-lined streets and town square, complete with a white gazebo, or our nearby farmland. It's like someone created this place while staring at a postcard of a utopian American suburb from the '50s.

Instead, the maggots are crawling into all the dark nooks and crannies. They tried to get a comment from Tom and failed. They tried to get shots from the crime scene and delivered a wall of tarp and tent. They got random man-on-the-street reactions, which all said the same thing: *There's a killer among us, and we're scared.*

Then they connected with Reverend Matthison, whose voice, as it always has, raised the hairs on my arms and neck.

He read from a paper all too familiar to me, one of his personalized sheets. The ones he prints his sermons on. His words flowed about the grace of his daughter and the evil of men. He vowed to help in every way possible and asked us to do the same. Then he ended with a quote from the Bible: "Dearly beloved, avenge not yourselves, but *rather* give place unto wrath: for it is written, Vengeance *is* mine; I will repay, saith the Lord."

We were on our phones then, checking what was being posted. I think we were also confirming what we were all thinking: *Don't fuck with Matthison.*

I head upstairs and put on my binder and feel more myself. At least on the outside. Inside is a different story. My heart's beating, my lungs are drawing air, but they must work against the heaviness of every thought. I can and cannot fathom what has happened to Mary.

I pull a hoodie on and check to see if Tyler's ready. He has dark circles under his eyes and seems to be drifting back to sleep on the couch. I pat his knee. "Come on, bud, it's going to be a long day."

Ten minutes later Beth hops in shotgun. She kisses me and says good morning to Tyler. He smiles but doesn't speak.

"You two look how I feel," Beth says as we drive to Charlie's.

I check on Tyler in my rearview mirror. He's slumped against the window. I slide my fingers into Beth's, and we both sigh.

Charlie flies out his front door and hops in the back with Tyler. He looks around, nods, and tucks into himself. It feels like he wants to say something but put it on pause for the moment. And so we all stay quiet until after Tyler extracts himself from my car and slouches toward the middle school.

"So, any suspects?" Charlie asks.

"Really? You're starting with that already?" Beth has pulled her hand from mine so she can grip the seat while she turns around to face Charlie.

"I am. Sorry." Charlie leans toward her. "It's the only way for me to feel less sad, you know, to try and do something. And *he's* the only one who can really add to the conversation."

But I can't. Not really. Not in the way Charlie wants to. Because it's fine when it's a random story about someone I don't know, or a case from *Forensics Files*, but this . . . Mary. I can't.

"So, Av, any thoughts?"

Out of the corner of my eye, I see Beth turn from Charlie to me. It feels as if she understands my dilemma. "Too many," I say. "And not one of them is any useful."

They both nod, which is a bit unsettling, but I grip the wheel and keep driving.

"Yeah. I get that," Charlie says. "But, I mean, it has to be one of them, Calder or Matthison. Last ones to see her alive."

"Charlie, not now." Beth's words slice off any more of what Charlie's thinking, and we're quiet the rest of the way in.

We pass reporters and TV news trucks, stationed across from the school. One of Tom's men stands with his arms crossed, watching kids cross the street and away from the hungry microphones. And then, in the parking lot, we see the flock.

They're outside the front door, holding hands and singing. I park and turn my attention toward them, looking for Calder. There's a uniformity about them I've come to expect, but today it doesn't exist. It's the first time I've seen them without Mary, and I'm almost unable to speak. Almost. "Calder's not here, Charlie."

Beth's breath catches, and Charlie presses to the window. "Knew it," he says.

We pass the congregation, and I keep my head down. Not that I need to today. Their eyes are closed in prayer.

The guidance counselors are all in the foyer. "If you need to talk at any time today, just come down. We have additional staff," one of them says to the students passing by. Then she looks at me and opens her mouth to utter that same line, I'm sure. But she stops. Her mouth hangs open. I step closer to her and her eyes bulge, then dart, looking for some help from her colleagues, or an escape route.

I turn and join up with Beth and Charlie, who are moving in the same direction as everyone else. There's only one spot in this school worth visiting today.

The shrine is like a construction site. Flowers and stuffed animals are flowing from Mary's locker, which is covered in an enormous framed picture of her, surrounded by paper, on which people have written messages.

"Avery?" Beth says, but I ignore her and walk through the crowd.

It parts, and whispers cover me as I squat and take in all the notes, all the sadness.

My eyes fill and I wipe them away. Beth's words are in my ear. "You want to write something?" Somehow she's found a marker and is handing it to me. But I don't take it.

"I'm curious, Avery. What you gonna write?" Eva's voice cuts the moment short. How did I not realize she wasn't with the flock outside?

I grab the marker out of Beth's hand. "Depends where I'm writing." I uncap the marker and look Eva over.

She shakes her head, and her braided pigtails flap around her neck. "Avery, Avery. Now's not the time for anger. Let's mourn and honor Mary's life."

There's a murmur of throaty "Amens" behind her.

I look at the marker in my hand. Eva's right. I'm going to have to deal with them and I'm going to have to get through this despite them. Because as much as I hurt, I have to admit that they were closer to Mary than I was. At least, recently.

I motion toward Mary's locker. "Can I?"

"Go ahead," Eva says, directing me toward the locker as if she's showing one of her prized pigs at the fair. Before I put marker to paper, I scan the crowd for Calder. He's not with this branch of the flock, either. Which means he's probably home today. Probably where I should have stayed.

Mary's picture is life-size. Standing next to it, with my elbow against the cool locker, my head angled to write, it feels as if I'm about to tell her a secret. But in school I never would have been able to get this close to her.

After our moment during that summer between eighth grade and high school, I never got as close to Mary again. Her dad pulled in the reins and kept her close. Even when I tried to say hello at school, the flock surrounded her and brushed me off. I would text and would sometimes get a response, until Reverend Matthison must have found her phone and texted back: *Go away!*

Outside of school was no different. She always had company. Her parents or the flock. Or Calder.

Never understood the two of them. I could never get my head around how the reverend was okay with a prick like him. Perfect on the surface, but an asshole beneath. I can't count the number of times he's called me out, telling me I'm a freak or a dyke or that God hates me. And in this town, this quaint little tree-lined street, gazebo-sporting middle-of-nowhere, he's in the majority. Which is why Mary never stood up to him. Or, at least that's what I tell myself.

I close my eyes and savor the moment for the moment it is—a rare opportunity to be close to her—and not what it isn't—a pathetic and artificial stand-in for the real girl. One of the Bible passages that I remember from the countless I heard or read in her home comes to mind. I don't remember where it's from or all the words, but I write: *While we look not at the things which are seen, but at the things which are not seen: for the things which are seen are temporal, but the things which are not seen are eternal.*

I turn and hand off the marker to someone who backs away at my mere presence. Eva's open-mouthed, gazing. "Fitting," is all she says.

Beth, Charlie, and I walk away. "You're going to be okay, Avery," Beth says as we near my locker.

"I know," I say, "just not today."

"None of us will," Beth says, hugging me, and then we part for class. Charlie and I head to forensics.

"Calder's got top spot," he says once we're out of earshot. And as much as I don't want to go down that road, not with Mary, I have to agree.

The bell rings and the class quiets. We wait for Mrs. Luce, who eyes us as she did when we entered, nervously. She looks around, frowns, and takes a deep breath. "I'm sorry, this is probably the most difficult day I've had as a teacher. I knew Mary and I cannot comprehend what has occurred."

Mrs. Luce looks over our heads, never quite meeting our eyes. She's lying. Not about this being difficult, but about the comprehension. She, above all—possibly even Tom and his men—knows exactly what has occurred.

"Well, my plan today, if you remember, was to investigate blood spatter." Luce pauses, and takes another deep breath. "However, in light of the tragedy, I didn't think that would be appropriate." Another pause. "Yet we must meet our lab requirements for course credit, and there's only so much time. Therefore, I've spoken with Principal Williams and he's agreed that whoever doesn't feel comfortable may go to the library and complete a packet I've prepared while the rest of you complete the lab with me."

The class squirms, and it feels like everyone is hedging a bet.

Mrs. Luce places a stack of papers on the front table. The packet is enormous. "Please, decide now."

No one moves. I look around and the class is solid, not wavering.

"Okay, then, partner up at your stations."

We move to the black lab tables, and Mrs. Luce hands out the materials. "Your job is to identify the types of spatter patterns and to explain how you know this is the type, as well as how each might have occurred." She slides a series of white tented cards our way. "Feel free to use your textbook as reference."

Charlie and I get down to it and in no time have identified the passive spatters, as well as the active, low, medium, and high velocity patterns by measuring the droplets, considering the angle of impact. Based on this we make guesses about the weapons, which range from a mostly harmless razor to a hunting knife to a bullet.

And then we stop because we hear this conversation around us: *You think they're doing this to Mary? Like, if she was stabbed or shot or something? I don't know, it's been raining. Does that change anything?*

Charlie looks me in the eyes, and his own dance in his head. He's trying to get a read. I don't know what he sees, but I stare back until he looks away. Then he scratches his beard.

"What are you thinking?" I ask.

He shakes his head and I wait, because I want to hear what's on his mind. He's smart. Almost as smart as me. "No. It's wrong what I'm thinking."

"You have no idea where my head's been."

He looks over at the other kids and at Mrs. Luce. "Okay. I, well, I guess, in a way, I kind of agree with them."

I cross my arms over my chest.

"I mean," Charlie continues, "they're right about the crime scene with the rain and all."

"But yesterday was beautiful, nothing but sun." I have a sense where he's going and so I know this point doesn't matter.

"Right, right." He turns away.

He's looking at our stupid assignment, but I know what he sees. It's the same as I've seen ever since Tom came to the door. "What do you have next period?" I ask.

"English. Why?" Charlie looks at me again.

"No, you don't."

His face clouds for a second, but then clears and is bright and horrified and excited at the same time.

"Can't hurt to look, right?"

"I have no idea," he says.

"Then let's find out."

Charlie nods, still looking at me like he's waiting for me to change my mind. But I don't intend to, and I don't know why I didn't think of it sooner. There are too many pieces up in the air, too many unknowns. Like the way Tom answered me when I asked if it was Mary. He didn't say yes. He said, "It has to be." If I hadn't been so overwhelmed, I would have pressed. And there's no way I can ask Tom what he meant now. I probably won't be able to get close enough to speak with my uncle until this case is over.

Case. That's what Mary's life is now. Something to solve. Something that demands justice. In a way, I wish I were Tom. At least then I could be the one to do for her what she deserves.

But since I am not him, the least I can do is help. How, I'm not sure. How that will work—investigating rather than mourning—can't possibly be the smart move. Fuck it. I need the full picture, not the shards that we've been left with. And not because of forensics, but because this *thing* that has occurred is more than just *about* Mary. It *is* her. I may not ever be able to let her go, but at least I can try to understand the unimaginable.

As we pull out of the school parking lot, I realize that even though I'm driving, I don't know where I'm heading.

"Hey, do you know where that road is?"

Charlie looks puzzled for a second. "Uh, yeah, yeah I do. Hang a left at Farmingham and then take that for like five miles to that red barn. It's just up from there."

I know the road. I think we used to get our Christmas tree out that way, but I'm not positive. "How do you know?"

"After the news on Sunday, I went home and was asking Dad about the spot because it sounded familiar."

I ignore the road and look at him. "Familiar, how?"

"You remember, back in fifth and sixth grade, Dad and I used to hunt. It was our thing. Before Mom got sick."

I remember, but only vaguely, a picture or two of Charlie and his dad with a deer and rifles. Mostly it's his poor mother I remember. No hair. Withered. Her funeral was the first I ever attended and it was terrifying. "Yeah, okay. What about it?"

"We used to use that road. I think it's an old logging site or something. Dad says a lot of people around here use it."

His words circle around my head, and I try to focus on the road but can't. "You realize what you just said, right?"

Charlie thinks. "No. What?"

"It's a known spot, easy to access. Why would someone leave Mar . . . a body there?"

Charlie stares out his window for a moment and we're both quiet. I remember him getting in the limo, going to his mother's funeral. He is staring now like he was then. He speaks, but keeps his eyes out the window. "He wanted her to be found."

I close my eyes at the thought and Charlie's word reverberates: *Found.* She's been found. But we're still searching for her killer. I open my eyes. "Like a game?"

"Yeah. Maybe." Charlie squirms in his seat. "I don't like that idea at all."

I turn onto Farmingham and my phone chimes. I hand it to Charlie. "Read it for me."

"It's from Beth. 'Where the hell are you?'" He frowns. "Shit. Do you think we should have asked her to come?"

"No. She would not be cool with this." Charlie nods, and I hate myself for the truth, for the fact that *I'm* barely cool with this, and that I know Beth, who already worries about my feelings for Mary, is going to come undone when she finds out what we're doing.

"What do you want me to text?"

I don't want to lie, that only makes it worse. "Tell her we're on an extracurricular trip."

"*Extracurricular trip?* Really?"

I throw up my hands. "I don't know. Text what you think will work."

Charlie sets to it, and I want to take my words back, as well as my phone. He smiles when he's done.

The *woosh* of Beth's reply sounds before I can ask what he said.

"Good news or bad news?" he asks.

"Pick."

"Okay. There is no good news. I just said that because you're supposed to. She said that if you weren't back at school in five minutes she's going to call Tom."

"Shit. What did you text her?"

"The truth."

I pull onto the shoulder and press my head into my steering wheel. I'm screwed. Beth doesn't make idle threats. And I really should have asked her to come, even if she wouldn't have wanted to. We've had that conversation before. I suck at asking and offering. And at discussing my feelings. I once tried the line, "It's a guy thing," and she hit me, saying that was bullshit and holding back your emotions was stupid for anyone.

"What do you want to do, Av?"

I sit back and shut off my car. "Give me the phone." He hands it over and I text: *I'm sorry. We just decided. I didn't think. Can't come back right now. I'll be back by end of the day. If you want to talk about it, we can. If not, ok.* I tack on a smooch face emoticon, but doubt it's going to help.

I watch the text bubble pop up, but after a moment it disappears.

Around my car are trees and bushes, the green flecked with yellow. We're in the woods. I look down the road. "How far away do you think we are?"

Charlie turns and looks. "Probably a half mile, not more."

"Good." I open my door.

"What are we doing?"

"Walking. Come on." I see his smile a second before he tucks it away. I love him for the fact that he tucks it away.

We walk and are quiet, because aside from the humming noise of the woods, voices are audible, as are the squawks of walkie-talkie communication. It feels like we're so close that any second we'll see a cop with a gun standing in the middle of the road, but I know from so much time in the woods that's not it; it's the echo. Well up ahead, the clearing is visible, as are slashes of yellow tape, cutting across the orange and red leaves. We stop and take it all in.

There are more cops out in these woods than I've ever seen around town. The place is crawling with them, talking, staring, taking notes. I can't find Tom but I'm sure he's here.

"You see the markers?" Charlie says pointing, but doesn't really have to.

The yellow numbered markers stand around a central location, reminding me of the old connect-the-dot worksheets we used to get in school. If I connected these, would Mary's outline emerge? That's an awful thought.

"They've got evidence," he says. I see what he means: detectives in gloves placing things in bags or jars with tweezers. We're too far away to be able to tell what's been found, but it's obvious that they're looking for more. There's a half dozen people, all focused on the ground. One is taking pictures, and another stands behind the kind of tripod I've seen on the side of the road.

This is where Mary lay. For a day? More? The entire week? Could it have been that long? I close my eyes, but that only welcomes more thoughts, keys me up even more.

I try not to think about the effects that the rain and sun and cold nights and warm days would have on an exposed body. Mary's body. But I know too much because of this stupid interest of mine. Why forensics and not engineering or something?

Because I find it fascinating, that's why. And so I know that she would have been bloated, with blood pooled to whatever part of her was on the ground. Her skin would have been purple and blue. If she was found after a day, rigor mortis would have passed. Her limbs would have been soft and loose. And the orifices, even her eyes, they'd be filled with insects, particularly maggots. With the warm days we've had, they would have populated, and there would be beetles joining in. If she's been out here a week, the destruction would be greater, with larger animals having taken notice of the stench and coming to dine. Parts would be missing, especially on her face.

I turn and dry heave. I can't help the reflex, but I know enough to stuff my shirt in my mouth to dampen the sound.

"Avery, shh." Charlie covers my mouth with his hand and I gag into my shirt. He grabs my shoulder and leans in. "Breathe through your nose. You'll be okay."

I do, and inhale through the slits of his fingers, and wait for an officer to arrive any second. I am still, and no one comes.

We're quiet, watching, waiting, and I take in the surroundings. We're in the middle of nowhere, but not nowhere to whoever brought Mary here. I elbow Charlie. He lets go, and I pop my shirt out of my mouth. "What do you think about the hunter, the one who found Mary?"

"Like, as a suspect?"

I nod.

"Good question. I mean, there are a lot of people who hunt out here, but *he's* the one who came here. Found Mary."

"Or did he?"

Charlie squints at me.

"All we know is what Tom said. That guy could have had her in his house or something, and then *brought* her here."

Charlie's eyes go wide. "Avery, listen to yourself. If that's the case, he'd be in jail. You know they searched his house after he found Mary. Tom's not stupid."

I don't know if I feel anger at the story I'm telling myself or if I'm upset because it's the right one, just with wrong parts.

"But what do I know, Av? Maybe he is a suspect, and Tom is just waiting to see what these guys find out. It's still early. You know how much *that* matters."

I do. Which is why I push past Charlie.

"Where are you going?" he whisper-yells at me.

"Stay there. Can't have both of us getting caught."

He growls something I don't hear, but it doesn't matter. His frustration doesn't come close to matching mine.

There are at least thirty people up ahead, every last one of them no doubt desperate to find a clue, to begin to fit the pieces into place. Or so I hope. And if they're not, well, at least Charlie and I will be thinking in the background, possibly informed enough to help. That is if I can get close enough.

Hiding is my thing, though. I'm an expert. I've hidden so much of myself for all these years, it's basically second nature. So I slip back out to the road, making damn sure to stay close to the trees and keeping my head on a swivel for any of the police scouting.

A few minutes later and the crime scene lies twenty feet away. No one has turned. They keep to their work, and I scour for a way to get closer. The sheer volume of them has worn a path through the leaves. It's a gamble, but if I'm careful, I should be able to walk it, soundlessly.

I hold my breath, peer around a tree, and chart my steps. I dart to the next tree, thankful for the damp ground. No leaves crunch. I move to the next, and then another, and in a few minutes I'm pressed against a tree trunk next to a parked cruiser.

I close my eyes. I listen. I try to see what they're seeing.

"I don't know how it connects. I'm no Bible expert." The voice is only a few feet away.

"But it has to connect," another voice replies. "She's the reverend's daughter."

I don't breathe. My heart stops beating just so I can listen better.

"Yeah." The first voice has turned, is facing me. "What was it again?"

The first voice takes his time. It sounds like he's flipping notes. "Luke 5:31–32."

I wait for them to say more, but they don't. As much as I don't want to move, because they might hear me, I have to.

I slide my phone out and then almost squeal because I have service. But I focus and go to the Internet. I type in the reference and click on the first link:

And Jesus answering said unto them, They that are whole need not a physician; but they that are sick. I came not to call the righteous, but sinners to repentance.

The words tumble through my head so hard that I almost miss the voices behind me, speaking again.

"Why in her mouth? Any significance?"

"Sure. Could be. But considering what else was done to the body, may have been a convenience thing."

The words of the Bible passage float before me, as do *mouth*, and *convenience*. I try. I try so hard not to see what I can, but it's too late. Mary, rain-soaked and bloated, covered in insects, a Bible passage about repentance in her mouth, and whatever else has been done to her body, lying in the open, unprotected and so vulnerable. I see it, and I feel her scream, the one I've heard before, and the one I wish she could have stopped this search with. But it's gone. She's gone. Some animal has taken her. Here in these woods, the evidence is everywhere. But is it screaming loud enough? Is it doing the job?

I don't know. Can't know. Won't know. And here I am, in hiding, always hiding, and it's not okay anymore. None of this is fucking okay anymore.

My body wants to scream, to cry out, to express its anger and frustration, but I can't let it. Not now.

"Hey, who's back there?" I hear behind me, from one of the cops who was just talking.

I freeze.

"Hey, answer, shithead."

I can't. Don't.

The audible crackle of the walkie-talkie pops. "Yeah, we have a possible situation near the road. All eyes on that twenty."

Uncle Tom has talked to Tyler and me for years about what to do in a situation like this. But I never imagined I'd actually be somewhere that would include the police arresting me, so I only vaguely listened. But I remember enough to show my hands when I step out from behind the tree.

"Hands up! Get your hands up!" the two cops scream in unison, and I notice their guns are drawn. Everything inside me goes cold.

"On your knees! Hands on your head! Now!"

I listen and kneel and wait for what I know is coming.

A second later, cuffs are strapped to my wrists, which are pinned behind my back. I'm kneeling in the middle of the woods, yards away from where Mary was murdered, and I suddenly feel more vulnerable than I have ever felt.

"What's your name? Why are you here?" I can't tell which cop is screaming or if it's both. They yell and I can't answer, so they pat me down. They frisk my sides and back, pull my wallet and my phone from my jeans, and ask if I have any weapons. I still can't answer, so they check my waistband and knock around the empty space at my crotch.

Cops appear behind them, but I don't see Tom. In the distance I hear screaming. "Down! On your knees! Put your hands on your head!"

They've got Charlie, too.

Another cop, one I vaguely recognize, grabs my wallet from the two officers and rifles through it. He looks at my license and then at me. "What are you doing out here, *Avery*?"

I don't answer. This time, though, it's not only the fear. I can't read the inflection he just used with my name. Does he know me?

"You're that freak, aren't you? Girl who's a boy or whatever. Tom's niece, right?"

I don't know what to say or how to answer, but I know I should speak. They're all staring at me. A dozen cops, hands still on their holsters, surrounded by trees dropping leaves, backlit by blue sky. And their eyes are as uniform as their purpose, filled with confusion.

"I am. I was friends with Mary. I just wanted . . ." I can't finish. I don't really know what I wanted.

The cop steps forward, leans an arm across his leg so he can speak to me. When he does, it's a raspy whisper. "A lot of people were friends with Mary. I highly doubt the two of you were that close. But what makes you so special that you think you can come out here? Is it because Tom's your uncle? Does that make you think you're even more of a snowflake?"

He doesn't wait for me to answer.

"And who's back there? What's the plan here, Avery? Trying to get pictures to sell to those reporters?"

The officer leans closer, and even though he couldn't be more wrong, I struggle with finding the words to say, because, *I just needed to see for myself* doesn't seem like it will help me. There's no way he'll ever understand.

"Is there something you want to tell me, Avery *Chase*?"

I've heard my last name as a curse more times than I can remember. But this one, tacked on to this question, turns a piece of me, somewhere inside that won't accept the attack.

"A lot of things. But something tells me you're too stupid to understand."

"You piece of . . ."

But then a hand grabs his shoulder, pulls him upright. Tom is attached to the hand.

"What is going on?" Tom asks, and it's unclear if he's asking me or the officer.

"Tom, I can explain."

Tom holds up his hand for me to stop. I do. "Officer Wright, fill me in."

"Your nie . . . Our men found Avery snooping around, but she hasn't said a word about why she's here." He says *she* like he's throwing jabs, and they sting just like he wants. "She did call me stupid, though."

Tom looks from Officer Wright to me. He clenches and unclenches his jaw and the vein on his forehead distends. I'm not sure *pissed off* covers this emotion.

"Avery, what the hell?"

I feel like a child again, standing in front of my uncle, who's asking me what I've done wrong. He's always been good at that, at catching me doing stupid things. But he has always been there for me. He's never once—at least never to my face—questioned where I stand. He taught me to throw punches while my parents talked to school officials about the bullies. Tom helped me perfect my swagger while he should have been patrolling his beat. He talked to me about sports and girls and about how not to be an asshole. He talked to me like a man. But in this moment I can see none of that matters. Because I haven't listened to all of the other advice. I've fucked up. Big. Time.

"I'm sorry," I say, and feel tears clawing up my throat. "I just . . . I wanted to . . ." I stop, or Tom putting his hand on my shoulder does. Either way, I wouldn't have been able to go on.

"Avery, you need to understand this. Right now. You cannot be here. Ever again. I know you want Mary's killer found as much as we do, but this doesn't help."

I hold back the tears trying to well into my eyes.

Tom dips his head so he can look me in the face. "Forget it all, Avery. Forget everything you saw here. Everything you heard. Because if you can't, it's only going to cause more harm than good." He pauses, squeezes my shoulder. "Okay, bud?"

I nod at the impossible, at the unreasonable, and then I look into Tom's eyes and I lie. "I promise."

CHAPTER 4

Dad places some homemade soup before me like it's any other weeknight. I think he believes that if I eat, then it will be just some regular evening around the dinner table, and not the aftermath of this afternoon. I stare at the liquid and see my reflection.

Tom drove us in his cruiser, while another officer took my car, so he could talk to us.

"I have to report this, Avery. I have to follow protocol." He looked at Charlie in the rearview mirror. "Which means you'll be mentioned, too, Charlie. Don't worry, I'll talk to your dad."

"Thanks, Tom," Charlie said, and in those two words, I felt how upset he was. Not only with me for dragging him along and getting him in trouble, but for the heap of shit I knew his dad was going to throw on him. Before Charlie's mom died, he was a much happier man. But in the years since she's been gone, he's gotten progressively worse. Angry, bitter, and not exactly thrilled with his son's choice of friends.

We pulled into Charlie's driveway and he got out. He didn't say a word to me. I watched him go in his house, and then his dad came out and stood on the porch. "That's my cue," Tom said, and went up to the house. Charlie's dad looked over at the cruiser once. That was enough. When Tom got back in, he said, "He understands. But don't push it. Give Charlie and his father some space."

We drove and I wanted to push everything. I wanted to ask all the questions, but I couldn't. I'd already done enough.

My Dad was in the driveway when we got there. My car and the officer driving it pulled in next to Tom's cruiser. Dad was beyond confused. Before Tom got out he said to me, "Let me handle this."

As if I had other options.

The other officer tried to stay, but Tom ordered him into the cruiser. "This is family business," he said. The cop's eye roll told me how much shit Tom's in for.

"Gordon," Tom said, "I got Avery and Charlie out of what could have been a very bad situation. Had I not been there, you might be picking him up at the station right now."

Dad shook his head as Tom explained the scene and how he had to call it in to his superior and get permission to bring us home. He didn't mention a single detail about Mary. He kept saying *investigation* and how we'd interfered with it. I don't know how he can disconnect like that. *Mary's murder.*

"Go inside," Dad said once Tom was finished.

I did, because anything else would have been futile.

Tyler was at the window when I came in. "Av, what the hell?"

I stared at him, stared at him how I wished I had stared at that cop.

Tyler came closer. "No, I meant, are you okay?"

I hugged my brother so hard I was afraid I'd hurt him. But I don't think either of us cared.

After my shower, Mom was home, glass of wine

in hand. Dad was finishing up talking to her. "Sit," she said.

I took a seat on the couch.

"Do you understand, Avery? Do you truly grasp what happened today?"

"More than you can imagine," I said.

She nodded. "Good. So let that be an end to it. Let Tom and his men do their job. They'll find the truth. They'll find him. You have to trust that."

And now there's my soup, and in the background, the TV, and reporters talking about the case. Someone saying that new evidence has been found, that police are chasing down leads.

The minestrone is thick and pieces stick to my teeth but I suck them down. *Why her mouth?*

I shake it away. I finish my soup. My family looks from the TV to me. We don't talk about it.

"Can I be excused?" I ask.

Mom and Dad look at each other. Then Mom shrugs.

"Okay," Dad says. "I'll put a plate in the microwave in case your appetite returns."

I barely hear him as I sprint to my room and my phone.

Can we talk? I text Charlie, because there's no way I'm going to text him an apology. This is too big for that. But he doesn't answer. So I text Beth the same. My phone rings a second later.

"What is going on, Avery? I texted you like a hundred times."

"The cops had my phone. Sorry."

There's silence. Then, "What?"

And so I explain. It takes a while, and as I tell the story I feel the guilt weighing down my words.

"Why, Avery? Why the hell did you do that?"

"I don't know," I say, because it's easy. The truth isn't.

"What about Charlie? Is he okay?"

"Yeah. He's not talking to me, though."

"Really? Shocker. You almost get me arrested and I'm not talking to you either."

I pull the phone away from my face and stare at the red button. It would be so easy to hang up, to not try, to let go and forget it all.

I return the phone to my ear. "What do you think I should do?"

"Besides apologize? I don't know. Give him time."

I imagine tomorrow, me in Charlie's driveway, picking him up for school. His dad comes out on the porch and stares like he did earlier. "Yeah. Okay."

Beth sighs. "Are you going to tell me?"

"Tell you what?" My head begins to throb.

"What you found."

The throb pounds, like the feet in the woods. They could be tapping my phone. They could be listening right now, waiting. But if they are, that's stupid, a waste of time. I've done nothing but go and look. It's not my fault they don't have anything. Or, don't know what they have.

"They found a Bible passage in her mouth. One about sinning and redemption."

"Shit."

"There's something else, too. Something about her body. I don't know. It could be nothing, but the way they were talking . . ."

"Stop, Avery. You have to stop."

"But you asked me."

"I wish I didn't."

The red button itches against my face.

"This is where I go, Beth. You know that. And this is Mary we're talking about. This is a motherfucking murder investigation. What do you want me to say?"

"I wish I knew," she says.

That makes two of us.

"I love you, Av. That hasn't changed. You made a mistake, but you did it because you care, because you still . . ." Beth doesn't finish, but we both know where she was going and I'm proud of her willingness to try.

"Love you, too. It's just so hard, Beth. You know what Mary did for me. And now she's gone, and someone's to blame, and I feel like I owe her this."

"I do and I don't know. I mean, how can anyone but the two of you *know*? And I get where you're coming from, Av. Really. But you don't *owe* her. There's no debt to be paid. You've done nothing wrong."

"Which is exactly why it hurts so much."

She breathes heavily, maybe crying, I can't tell. "Tomorrow's a new day. Wait and see. Something good will come. Charlie will forgive you. Get some sleep."

I hope she's right. "I'll dream about you," I say, and hope that by saying it I'll will it into being.

Because if it's possible to feel a nightmare coming, then I do.

❖

I never did get my appetite back, and I never said good night to my parents. I texted Charlie again. He didn't reply. I opened my window and sat on the roof and smoked a cigar and stared at the woods. Through the night, under a thick blanket of moonlit clouds it was eerie and all the more ominous when I considered what had been done out there, under a cover of rain, a shower that washed so much away.

I didn't undress, didn't want to feel any more exposed than I felt today. Those hands were on me as I drifted off, searching, looking, trying to understand what was there.

Now my phone has woken me. It's pressed into my hand, as if I was waiting for this, for Charlie to finally get back to me. The buzz tingles as I clear my eyes to read.

Did you get the message?

I don't know how I missed Charlie's message. I try to scroll, but realize there's no history. This is one message. From a number I don't know.

I stare, confused.

Are you there?

My brain starts working, starts grasping the details. It's not as if I've never been taunted before. I'll just block this number. My finger hovers, about to bring me to Settings.

Luke 5:31–32

My hand freezes and my heart stumbles.

Little birdie saw you today. Heard you getting in trouble.

I rub my hands over my face, give my cheek a slap, make damn sure I'm awake and am really seeing this.

And so you must know. You must know. You must KNOW!

I pull it together and type. *Know what?*

You are there! You must know that the message isn't for them. It's for you.

I try to recall the scripture, but I only read it once, so it's vague. Whoever's on the other end of this exchange reads my mind.

And Jesus answering said unto them, They that are whole need not a physician; but they that are sick. I came not to call the righteous, but sinners to repentance.

In the words I see myself. I understand. It's the same as the officer earlier. *Freak. Sinner.* Synonymous.

What do you mean? My fingers fumble as I type.

Don't play dumb, Avery. REPENTANCE!

I'm sick at the thought, at the conclusion I've come to. *You killed Mary so I would repent?*

No. Because she refused to.

The words are insane, more disgusting than I think I can comprehend. He's admitted what he's done, that he killed Mary. Because? Because she wouldn't repent. For what? What could she have possibly done?

The answer comes before I can reply.

Because she loved you.

I flip my phone over so I don't have to look, so I don't have to stare at words that I already knew, but that now shift some of the blame to me.

But it doesn't help. The light still pours out the sides, and then my phone chimes with another message. I don't want to look. I don't want to know any more. But I don't have a choice. The killer is reaching out, providing the evidence Tom needs, that we all need.

So now you must repent.

There's an unsettling logic to this conversation, one that I understand from years of being Mary's friend. It's what provided me the words to write on her locker, and it's what guides me to this question now. *Or else?*

This town cares about Mary and it took one week to find her. How long do you think they would take to find you?

CHAPTER 5

I didn't call Tom. I didn't call 911. I didn't tell my parents I received a death threat. Instead, I silenced my phone and I stared out the window until dawn. On and off, I re-read the text exchange, trying to decipher a deeper message or clues to who it might be, but nothing emerged, except the sun.

So I don't know what this says about me. Do I not care about my life? Or am I being smart, waiting to see if this is just another prank. Because once I show Tom, he can't unsee what's there. He has to act.

There's a soft knock on my door and then Tom is moving into my room, holding two mugs of coffee. After a sleepless night this feels dreamlike.

"Tom?" I lean to the side and try to see his face when he turns. I do, and yesterday comes back, and I know I'm not dreaming.

"We need to talk."

"I know," I say, taking a coffee from him. We both sip our coffee and stare at nothing. I can only imagine what he's seeing behind those eyes.

"Yesterday," Tom begins. "Yesterday can never happen again."

I nod.

"No. Say it. Say that it will never happen. I need to know that you get it."

"Get what?"

Tom clenches his hand around the mug handle. I watch the middle knuckle go white. "Get that what you did could have landed you in jail. Get that I kept you out of there. Do you know how important that is?"

The evidence burns under my leg, but I don't care. Let it singe all the way through. I want to hear about what I owe.

"Of course," I say. "Who wants to go to jail? But we didn't do anything. We were just there. I told you that yesterday."

"Jesus Christ, Avery, I know!" Tom slams his mug onto my desk and lurches toward me. "I spent pretty much all of last night getting my ass chewed off by my boss. If the media catches wind that you were there, the next headline will read 'Crime Scene Tampering.'"

Tom settles back and looks away. I feel a twinge of guilt. The pressure he's under is immense.

"Okay. So what do you want?"

"I'd prefer that you stay out of everything. I know what Mary meant to you, to this town, but I have to ask that you think about what might happen before you do something stupid. My protection only reaches so far." He pauses. "You don't want to know where it ends."

I shake away the images that his words make me see, echoes of my past. Not having a penis hurts. And the way the world wants to remind me of that, even more so.

I look down into my mug. "I am sorry. And please don't blame Charlie. I took off on him. He didn't know what I was doing."

Tom sighs. "I figured as much. Don't worry, he's fine, like I said, so long as nothing shakes loose." He pauses. "Do you even know what *you* were doing?"

"I just wanted to take a look. You don't understand."

He sits on the corner of my bed. "Again, I know how you felt about Mary. And I know a lot about death and what it does to people. Especially murder. I can put two and two together."

I reach for my phone. It's time to help him find something.

His radio crackles. The voice on the other end asks for him. "What's your 10–20?" Tom's face shutters and he answers the call.

"Twelve East End. Over."

"We've got a possible 10–35 at Five Country Line," the dispatcher says. "What's your ETA?"

"Five minutes. Over."

Tom releases the walkie-talkie and stares ahead. I know that a 10–35 is a major crime and that the address where it's occurring is Mary's.

"Tom," I say, trying to explain what I should have as soon as he got here. Those texts. But it's not even eight in the morning and shit is hitting the fan at the Matthisons'.

And then he's gone, and I'm left in my room with his mug of coffee and a growing fear that whatever is occurring out there is connected to what sits on my phone, here. I'm afraid to leave. I'm afraid to stay. But I know I can't hide. Not anymore.

I pull into Charlie's driveway, full of things I must tell him: the texts, Tom's abrupt leaving and what it could be, that I'm sorry.

His dad steps out the door and onto the porch. He shakes his head.

It takes a moment for me to comprehend what's going on. And then my stomach bites itself and I pull back into the street. Charlie's dad goes back inside, shutting the door behind him.

I punch the steering wheel and yell, "Fuck!" And then I do it again because it feels good, necessary. Because sharing with him would have made things right, I know it. Charlie can see through the bullshit that sometimes I can't. But now I have to wait, and who knows what will be by the time we get to speak.

I go to grab my phone, to text him, but decide against it and leave it in my pocket. I pull away so fast that my tires squeal and head to Beth's.

Beth climbs in. "Where's Charlie?"

"His dad won't let him come out and play." I don't look at Beth when I speak, and as soon as she has her seat belt on I peel out.

"Whoa, whoa! Slow down."

But I don't. I speed up. I stare at the stop sign down the road and I make it my target. I floor it and look at it and only it until I'm at the intersection. When I look down the adjacent streets, cars are idling, ready to move forward. Beth screams, and I do not stop.

We fly through the intersection, car horns blaring, brakes squealing, and I finally breathe.

"Pull over now! Right now, Avery!"

I do. I was going to before she yelled. Once I'm on the shoulder, Beth jumps from the car. She pulls her bag behind her and starts walking down the street. I put the car in park and rest my head against the steering wheel. Both my doctor and my therapist have warned me about what testosterone can do. I've seen the physical effects and have loved them. But this? Can I blame this on that, or is this on me?

I get out of the car and run to catch up with Beth. "I'm sorr . . ." The punch comes before I can finish. I reel back and fall on my ass. Beth stands over me, seething.

"You want to act like an asshole, fine. But not with me." She kicks my leg and I hear a crunch.

"Okay, okay! Stop." I put my hands over my head.

"Stop? Are you kidding me? That's what *you* should have done. What the fuck is wrong with you?"

I pull my phone out of my pocket so I can show her. The screen is cracked from her kick, but I still have power. A little. I pull up the texts and hold my broken phone out to Beth. "Here. Read these."

Beth jerks the phone out of my hand as if what she's about to read is meaningless. I understand. This isn't the first time I've gotten some weird, rando, text threat. I usually share them with Beth, and so I understand where she's coming from. Why should this one be any different? Why should this justify what I just did?

"Avery, what is this?" Her voice is panicked, no longer angry.

"That happened last night."

"Did you call the police? Your uncle?"

"No."

"What? Why?" She crouches next to me, her own phone out. "You have to. Now. Right now." She looks down at my phone again. "You do realize what this is?"

"Of course I do. It's not my first death threat. But I can't call Tom now, he's at the Matthisons'."

Beth's face smooshes in the way my brain feels. "What the hell are you talking about?"

"Tom was at my house this morning to talk about yesterday."

"And you didn't tell him then?"

I hold up my hand. "Please. Let me finish."

Beth tightens her lips and lets me go on.

"I was about to. I had my phone in my hand. But then he got a call to go to the Matthisons'."

"What for?"

"I don't know. But he was gone before I could say anything. And after what I did yesterday, I don't trust anyone else."

Beth tilts her head, her face gone curious. "You've got evidence. They're not going to care about anything besides that."

I look away, down the street at my car. "You weren't there. You don't know. This one cop, Wright, I think. I could just tell what he thought of me."

"What do you mean?" Beth's voice is close, but I'm drifting back into yesterday, so it sounds far away.

"He kept using *she* on purpose. He knew who I was."

"Shit." Beth wraps her arms around me. "Why didn't you tell me this yesterday? You don't have to take that."

I don't give in to her affection. "But I do. For Tom. For the investigation. I can't let what I did mess it up."

"And what did you do? You went to the scene. You looked around? Who gives a shit? Read those texts. I think you're in the clear for snooping. I think if you want to do something for the investigation you turn this over. Stop second-guessing yourself, Avery."

I breathe deep. She doesn't know everything I do. My past is not her past, and it has to stay that way. Her being with me has already made her enough of a target. I don't need to make the circles brighter. "To Tom. Only him."

"Okay. I understand. But that means we reach out to him now. You're not safe."

"And neither is Charlie and he doesn't know that."

Beth's eyes go wide. "You don't know that."

I turn to her. "You read what those texts said. You know that whoever sent them was there yesterday. There's no way they could have known all that."

"True. Or someone there talked."

I shake my head. "If that's the case, and it gets out, I'm screwed. And so is Charlie."

Beth frowns. "If what gets out? That you were there?" She looks me over. "What aren't you telling me?"

"I can't. Not now." I grab her hand, hoping she understands I need her to let this go. "Please."

It takes a moment, but she squeezes back. "Okay. We get Charlie. We go to Tom. Period."

"Okay. But how? His dad doesn't want me near him."

"That's his issue. You don't know what Charlie thinks."

"He didn't return any of my texts."

"Well, he returned mine." She slips her phone into her hands and starts tapping away. I watch her hands but still have trouble understanding how they connected with Charlie and mine didn't.

Beth looks at me, smooths my hair, and says, "I'm still pissed about what you just did. You're not off the hook." She grips my hair. "But I kind of want to take that anger out on the cop from yesterday." Beth smiles in the way she first did, the way that let me know she was interested. I didn't know a year ago what that meant. How she saw me. What she liked. I do now. Somehow it's all of me.

Her phone sounds with a reply. She reads and then looks up. "Poor kid. He had to take the bus."

"So he's at school?"

"Yeah. Thoughts?"

School nurses have unbelievable bullshit detectors. In order to get him out, it's got to be good. I check the time on my cracked phone. First period is about to begin. It's early enough to make what I'm thinking work. "Tell him to get a big water bottle and sneak it into the nurse's bathroom."

Beth starts typing, then stops. "What?"

"I'm not done. He needs to barge in there, make a lot of noise. Then he has to wait. Wait until she knocks. Then he's got to make noise like he's puking and unleash the bottle into the toilet."

Beth stares at me. "For real?"

"It's worked before."

"That's sad, Avery." But she starts typing.

While she does, I think about how this could go, about what Tom is up to, about what happened in the woods, those texts, that scripture. And more than anything else, I think about Mary. I remember so much about her, the perfume she wore, the way her hair fell, the way she held her nose when she went underwater. And I remember the way she treated me. How she held my hand, rubbed the buzzed hair at my neck, didn't ask about my parts, only me. And the last thought produces a chill, because I think of what the cops said yesterday, about what else was done to the body. To Mary.

She's gone, not yet buried, and I didn't think that it could get worse. But what happened yesterday has reminded me all too well about how evil this world can be. How a girl can be taken and what, tortured? Mutilated? Worse? Then killed. Then hidden for a week.

And how someone like me—because of who I am and what they don't see—could be next. And how, in some fucked-up way, that wouldn't be as bad.

CHAPTER 6

I pull up to the front of the school and park.

"All right, I let him know we're here," Beth says, and sets down her phone.

"Thanks," I say and look at her.

"For what?"

"That hook of yours." I test my jaw. "Have you been working out?"

Beth shrugs. "Maybe." Then she leans closer. "I don't think it's good that I had to do that, but I'm glad I did if it knocked some sense into you. What was that? You don't even like *The Fast and the Furious.*"

"Yeah, it wasn't about the car. And it certainly wasn't about you." I have to look away. "Maybe Charlie's dad is basically telling me to go fuck myself? Or more likely that someone wants to kill me."

"And what about Mary? How does she factor here?"

I look back at Beth and try to place what I heard in her voice. Sympathy? Irritation? Concern? "What do you mean?" Beth knows only pieces of what I had with Mary, not the full picture.

She touches my face. "Don't, Av. Not with me. Don't bob and weave just because I'm asking about her. You loved her. I know. And that's fine, wonderful even. But you haven't said anything to me about that, about how much this must hurt. You can. I think you should."

I close my eyes and Beth rubs my neck, and it's almost too much, too similar to the hands of the girl she was just talking about, whose hands were the first to be here. And whose body is now gone. Beth's right, a piece of her is still with me. But how do I talk about that? And how can I sit and mourn her, when there's work to be done? Her killer's out there, literally begging to be found. Or ready to strike again.

I open my eyes and I look directly into Beth's. "Losing her hurts more than not being who I am meant to be."

Charlie rattles into the backseat, breaking up our moment. He doesn't sit back, though. Rather, he lies on the floor. "Go, Av!"

I don't ask questions, I drive. A couple of blocks later Charlie pops up. "Coast clear?"

"Yeah," I answer. "Why didn't you go to the nurse's like we told you?"

"No. That would have worked and all, but then she would have called my dad to pick me up and he's already pissed at me, so I just walked out."

"What?" Beth turned around in her seat.

"Yeah. Foster's probably marking me absent for chem right now." He smiles.

"What's going on with you?" I ask.

"Really? That question?" Charlie groans. "You remember what happened yesterday?" I nod. "Yeah, Dad's pissed at you, so I couldn't text back. He checks the history. But he doesn't really know who Beth is, so I just lied and said you were helping me with homework." He pats her headrest. "Thanks for the help with that essay. Really top notch."

Beth laughs and turns back around. "Anytime."

"And so we're here now. What are we doing?" Charlie asks.

"I thought you told him," I say to Beth.

"Hell no. I'm not texting all that. Give him your phone."

I pull my phone out of my pocket and stare at the cracked screen for a second.

"What happened?" Charlie asks.

"She did."

Beth gives a little wave.

I toss the phone back to him and tell him to read the texts. Charlie grabs the phone and navigates around the broken screen. He holds up his hands and says. "Uh, it's dead. Plug it in to your charger."

"I don't have one."

Beth rifles through my glove compartment to see if I'm wrong. "You and your damn cigars. What are we going to do with it now?"

"I can still give it to Tom. He'll just have to plug it in."

"We're going to the police station?" Charlie asks, and I feel like I should pull over just so we could all talk and get on the same page, especially Charlie and me. But there's no time for that.

Like yesterday, there are cops everywhere. But now, their cruisers are blinking, lights whirring, and yellow tape encloses most of the Matthison property.

"What happened?" Charlie asks.

I pull over down the road, near where the neighbors have gathered and the reporters are assembling.

If we have any chance of blending in, this is it. I take in the scene and see familiar signs from yesterday. Evidence markers, baggies, men scouring the ground. Tom is talking with a group of officers. One of them is the asshole from yesterday. I grip the steering wheel.

"Matthison's a suspect?" Charlie says, leaning over the seat to get a better view.

"Why do you say that?" Beth asks.

"The evidence markers. They're collecting."

"Yeah, but Mary lived here. That makes sense, right?"

I think about Beth's point. Maybe it does. But if it doesn't, then Charlie's onto something.

"Charlie. Yesterday. How much did you hear?"

"About you or about the case?"

Beth looks between us, but her eyes settle back on me. She says nothing.

"Both," I say.

"All of what that cop said to you. He wasn't holding back on using *she*. But next to nothing about Mary." He grips my headrest. "That's him, isn't it?" Where he's pointing is spot on. It's Officer Wright.

I nod.

"So what did *you* hear?" Charlie asks.

I look down because the words want to leap out and I know I have to get them straight first. Tom doesn't want me talking about this. What I know can't go past here. But if I can't trust my best friend and my girlfriend to keep this secret, who can I trust? They're the best people I have ever known aside from my family and Mary.

I say a little prayer for forgiveness and then I speak. "Something was done to her body. I don't know what, but I heard the cops talk about it, that something had been done." I can feel both Beth and Charlie wincing at my words. "But there's more. There was a note left in her mouth."

"What? What did it say?" Charlie grips the seat harder.

I turn to Beth. "Do you remember the Bible passage from the texts?"

She nods and then her eyes widen and she brings a hand to her mouth.

"What, Avery? What was it?" Charlie's practically sitting on my dashboard now.

"It was a passage about repentance. And last night whoever texted me must have been at the scene. He mentioned what happened, and he texted the exact passage they found in Mary's mouth."

Charlie's too shocked for words. His face is stuck, much like Beth's. A cold realization slides into me: *I should fear for my life.*

"He said that if I don't repent, I'm next."

Charlie looks down, sees my phone, and holds it up like it's an injured bird. Then his face clears and he holds it tighter, looks out the windshield. "Then we get this to Tom." He turns back to me. "And you. You will never be out of sight. Never alone. I don't care if I have to camp out in your hallway."

A smile doesn't do justice to how I feel, so I reach out and grab Charlie, pull him to me, and hug so tight I feel his back crack. It reminds me of after his mother's funeral. Before now I've never felt so undone. Charlie, though, he was worse. She was everything to him and to his father. And somehow he trusted me, even then, to hold him like I am now. And like then, he doesn't resist, doesn't squirm like my brother. He means what he said, and he hugs me right back.

I don't know how I got so damn lucky to have these two in my life. And I sure as hell have no idea why Mary was so good to me. A reverend's daughter with the transgender kid. But it was fine. Is fine. Even though it's not. Because we wouldn't be here like this if she hadn't met me, if she hadn't felt what she did. But Mary lived by her heart more than she lived by the Bible passages that are cross-stitched and hanging on every wall in her home. That's what matters. And that's exactly how I must move forward.

Beth takes the phone out of Charlie's hand. "I got this," she says. I open my mouth to protest, but she stops me. "They know both of you. Do you really think they're going to let you near Tom?"

She's right.

"So, I'm going to march this right on over. Pathetic boys in their dress-up clothes still can't resist." Beth unbuttons the next two buttons on her shirt, and her very endowed chest is on display.

We've joked before about the irony of me loving her boobs so much, when I have my own pair that I hate.

Charlie and I both stare as she goes, because there's nothing we can do.

And sure as shit the cops turn, seemingly irritated that someone is walking up to the scene, but then they do a double take when they see her. It's gross, but at least this is her intention, to pull on their heartstrings. Some move toward her, others frown and shake their heads. One looks so pissed at the intrusion I think he's going to do to her what they did to Charlie and me yesterday. Then I see the realization hit Tom. His head snaps up and then it swivels from her to the crowd. He's looking for me, I know it.

Tom breaks away from his conversation and inserts himself with authority between his men and Beth. The men walk away.

Charlie and I watch as Beth pulls out my phone and gestures Tom closer. He bends and listens and then his spine stiffens as if he's been shot in the ass. He puts out his hand. Beth places the phone in his palm. Tom looks at it while Beth says more, and then he tucks it into the pocket of his shirt. He speaks to her and she nods like a thousand times, and then she walks away, back to us.

When she gets into her seat, she buttons back up and says, "Tom said to get your ass to school. There are two officers on duty, and he's telling them to keep you there until he comes for you."

"It's true, Av. I saw them before I took off," Charlie says.

"Was he pissed? Am I in trouble?"

Beth sighs. "No, Avery. He's afraid for your safety. You're his nephew."

"Did he say that? Did he say *nephew*?"

Beth shakes her head. "No. But that's not the point."

It's not, but I would have loved for that asshole to hear Tom say it. To say *nephew*. To mean me. To put that dick in his place. There may be time for that still. For now, I need to stay alive.

Tom wasn't kidding. One of the officers meets us as we enter school. He has a copy of my schedule, and my principal is with him, but has clearly taken a back seat to this man's authority. He didn't ask any of us for passes, and it's already lunchtime.

"Avery, I'm your shadow. If you need anything, give me a sign." The cop, Officer Howard, nods, so I nod back, and then we all make our way toward the cafeteria.

The bell rings and the halls fill with kids. They see me with a cop and our principal and gawk. I don't really blame them.

"Get your things and get to class," Principal Williams yells and kids scatter, but not before pictures are snapped.

Seeing their phones makes me think of my own and I wonder if Tom is charging it now and what will happen when he reads what's there. Will they be able to trace the number and catch the killer that quickly? That would put this nightmare to rest. But the waking truth of it all is that Mary is still gone. Her funeral is tomorrow. Killer caught or not, that's still going to happen.

Which makes it no surprise that the flock isn't eating. Rather, they're standing in the corner, leading a prayer circle, letting in all who want to participate.

"He's here," Beth says and points at the circle.

I don't need to question who she means. It can only be one of the two who last saw Mary alive: Calder Riley.

He stands, head down, hands linked with the group. I see them sneaking looks at him. I see them wanting to be a part of his pain. Was it him who sent those texts? And if so, how? How would he know what happened to me? If he's the killer, he knows more than anyone. But still, he'd have to know someone who was there yesterday.

"Dude, you stare any longer and they're going to think you want to join, or this guy's going to ask you who he should be arresting," Charlie says, while pointing at Officer Howard.

"You're right. Shit. It's just, it's just the first time seeing him. Top candidate and all."

Charlie shuffles along next to me, into the lunch line. "Maybe. Based on those texts, what you said."

I finish the thought for him. "He'd need to know someone."

Charlie scratches his beard. "You and me have some thinking to do."

"Shut up with that for right now," Beth says, and we do, maybe because of the presence of the cop, or maybe because of the prayer circle, or maybe because we realize we're not actually detectives.

Lunch is as awkward as it is for me to pee standing up. Sure, I can manage it at home without eyes on me, or here in the separate handicap bathroom, but this feels like when I'm out and the toilets are nasty and squatting is not an option. Eyes are on me, watching, wondering, trying to figure out what the fuck is going on. There's a cop leaning against the cafeteria wall watching over me like a bodyguard. School has always made me feel vulnerable, but this is over the top.

So we eat, and don't talk, and I hope for the day to fly by. But my prayers are never answered.

Eva, head of the flock, pride of the 4-H, country girl simple, sits down across from me. She looks at us all, but I know it's me she's come for. It's like if she converts me to her religion, she gets a golden ticket to heaven.

"Please join us. We're praying for Mary's soul and for Calder, who's back and needs our support." She pauses and puts her hands to her chest. "He's just heartbroken."

Beth is staring at Eva as if she'd like to try out her hook again. Charlie's ignoring her presence. I try to do the same but she grabs my hand.

"Come over with us, Avery. I know you're hurting, too. We can pray for you as well."

It takes effort, but I pull my hand away. "Really? You'd do that for me?"

"Of course. We pray for all sinners."

I shouldn't do this, but after yesterday and this morning, I simply cannot deal with one more issue.

"Do you pray for the killer? Do you pray for the one who took Mary's life? Huh? Him too?"

The room seems to hear the sharpness of my tone, or perhaps they've been waiting for it, because all eyes are absolutely on us now.

Eva shakes her head. "Avery, you poor thing. You have to learn how to deal with that anger in a positive way. But you won't be able to until you respect who you really are."

I lean forward and enjoy the edge of the table cutting into my stomach. I've long since lost my appetite. "And who is that? Who am I, Eva?"

She reaches for my hand again, but I pull it away. Officer Howard stands straight and this catches her eye. She looks over and then back at me. "Hmm," she says and then nods, "you are a lost soul, Avery. You are lost without God. If you accepted Him into your heart, then you wouldn't be so confused. You would see as clearly as we do, and your heart would know how to make the right choice."

Charlie sets down his sandwich. "I'm going to help you make a decision right now, Eva. Get the fu . . ."

I put up my hand, cut him off. I don't want this battle, but this is my battle. I stare at Eva, into her plain and blissful face.

"I've made my choice, Eva, and it's to never listen to you or let the stupid flock tell me who I'm supposed to be."

"Well, maybe someday you'll change your mind. We'll pray for you." She stands to leave, and I should let her go, but I can't. I can't because she is the embodiment of everything that religion is not about. I know this because of Mary.

"You know who never judged me, who never told me I should be something I'm not?"

Eva waits for me to answer my rhetorical question like someone who's watching a dog take a shit.

"Mary. The *reverend's* daughter. She understood. Her eyes were clear. She could actually see."

Eva looks up and then shakes her head at me. "And look what happened to her, Avery. Mary was looking at you with human eyes, not God's." She turns on her heel and rejoins the flock. Calder raises his head at her presence. I lock eyes with him and look for the hatred, but all I see is pain.

CHAPTER 7

I asked Officer Howard if I could leave, but he told me no, that Tom was personally escorting me. Which sounds insane, but he's done it before. Back in the early years, around third or fourth grade, when kids started hating on me because my hair was short and I passed as one of the boys so easily some actually forgot, Tom had to step in when they remembered. Because they did what kids do, find a target and keep practicing their aim until it is perfected.

The first time it was real bad, Tom stepped in. That day, he was at the classroom just before the last bell rang. My teacher opened the door and he smiled as he greeted her, but once he was past, and she was at his back, his eyes iced over. The entire class saw it and jumped. That was his goal. He then looked at me and over the members of the flock. Tom nodded and I needed no other instructions. I got my things and marched up the aisle, where Tom stood, wrist casually resting on his holster.

I felt so safe then, so protected that I flipped off Eva. Her eyes shot brimstone back. And that night I didn't have any nightmares. But the next day, the target on my back was like a magnet. Payback really is a bitch.

So now I have to wait. Beth's taking advantage of the time to make up a test, so Charlie and I slip into Mrs. Luce's classroom. She's at her desk, staring at her computer screen.

"Boys, hey, there's no forensics meeting today." She stops herself. "But you knew that. What's up?"

"Can we just chill here until my uncle comes? He's not letting me leave without him."

Luce pushes back from her desk. "Tom?" I nod and she pulls her face back as if trying to tuck it into her neck. "Is everything all right, Avery?"

How do I answer that question?

"Yeah. He's just being overprotective."

Luce nods madly. "Right. Sit, sit. I'm just going to finish . . ." She looks at her computer as if she's never seen it before. "This."

"It's okay, Mrs. Luce," Charlie says. "Thanks for letting us in."

She returns to her work, and Charlie and I settle into the desks.

"So, you want to make a list?" he says.

"You mean like actually write down a list of suspects? That's crazy. We lose that and we'll be added to it."

"Okay, okay. Solid point. We'll talk it through."

I try to get comfortable in my seat, but school chairs aren't really designed for comfort. "You know, we may not even need to make a list. Tom's got my phone. He traces that number. Bam!"

Charlie shakes his head. "It's been like three hours. Don't you think if he had anything, we'd already know? Those reporters and their stupid vans would all be rushing to the dude's house, whoever it is. We'd hear about that."

He's right. I don't like it, but that's some strong logic. "Yeah. Shit. So, Calder, right?"

"Absolutely. And Matthison." Charlie puts up his hands. "I know, that's sick, but the cops were at the house today. Might still be."

"But that could be nothing. What Beth said. But, okay, Calder and Matthison. Who else?"

"What about that hunter? I know I dismissed him, but he still could be. Seems less of a coincidence, not like some poor jogger finding a body. You know?"

"Yeah, good point." I lean back and need to itch under my binder. These things don't breathe nearly as much as they should. I reach in and dig under my left boob.

Charlie watches. "You want me to get that?" He laughs; he is the only one aside from Beth who gets to do that.

"Only if you'll let me borrow your package," I say.

Charlie leans in all serious. "Who told you it was detachable?"

I snort as I laugh and hear Luce clear her throat, so I simmer down. "Hey, Charlie, sorry about yesterday. I just took off. I didn't think it would go down that way."

"I know, man. But that's your thing, you don't always think it through. Just don't do it again, because arguing with my dad about you sucks. And I really don't want to go to jail, either."

I want to press the point about why it sucks so bad arguing about me, but now's not the time. He's forgiven me. Plus, he's right about me not thinking.

I know this about myself. But knowing about it and doing something about it are totally different.

"So, anyone else?" I ask.

Charlie looks down at his hands. "Depends. I don't think it's someone outside of town."

"Why's that?"

"Those texts. He's still here, watching."

The way he says *watching* makes my throat constrict. "So he has to be close to someone on the force."

Charlie's eye's pop. "Damn. Yeah. That's twisted."

"Officer Chase," Luce says behind us and we look up.

He smiles and steps into the classroom. "You mind if I take these two off your hands?"

Luce is on her feet. "They're never a bother. Without them we wouldn't even have a club."

Tom keeps smiling, but I see how thinly stretched it is. We've got to go, to talk. I need to hear what he has to say, not listen to Luce flirt with my uncle.

He turns to go, but Luce steps in his way. "Any development? Any at all? The school's been buzzing about something at the reverend's."

Tom runs a hand through his hair. "You know I can't talk about it. But I will say, watch the news tonight. We're getting closer."

This is excellent news, and I feel a sudden surge of hope. As does Luce, apparently. She hugs Tom. Then Charlie, Tom, and I head into the hall.

"So, closer?" I say.

Tom keeps walking. "It's a relative term."

Charlie and I shoot looks at each other, but then keep pace with Tom, as he heads toward the entrance. Beth is there, watching the news vans that seem to have followed Tom's car. She turns when she hears his boots, and her face screams the question I believe only Tom can answer.

My uncle glares at the vans for a minute and then turns back to us. "Thank you for this," he says, and holds up my phone. He looks over at Beth. "Nicely done."

She smiles but I watch the phone, wait for what's next, the reveal.

"Here's the deal. Unfortunately, I need more. I need you to get a new phone so that in case this guy reaches out to you, you actually have a phone that works."

I wait for more. Nothing comes. "So, did you trace the number? Do you know who it is?"

"I can't answer those questions, Av. You know that. Sorry. But if you think it through, you'll realize if I need more, then we're not there yet."

"So what about the Matthisons'? What about what you said to Luce?"

He puts his hand on my shoulder. "I just said we're closer. We are. There will be coverage on the news. Watch it. But that's it for now."

I squirm under his hand. I want more, need more, but this is a dead end. "So what about my shadow? What do I say to my parents?"

"Already talked to them."

No angle there, either. I just want to crack his veneer and peek inside.

"How am I supposed to pay for a phone?"

Tom reaches into his pocket and pulls out two crisp one-hundred-dollar bills. "Compliments of the force."

I take them from him without a word. If he notices my irritation, he doesn't show it. Instead, he turns to the officer who's been following me around. "Officer Howard will take your old phone from you when you're done."

"Why?" I ask, just to ask.

"It is now part of the investigation." Tom leans closer to me. "Avery, I know you wanted this to be over, for us to have found him. I did, too. But this isn't as easy as they make it seem on TV. We need time, and all the evidence we can get. Some jerk here might be punking you."

I go to speak, but he talks over me.

"Or it could be the real deal. And based on the evidence, I'm truly concerned about the latter. Hence your protection."

I let the words sink in. I listen before reacting. Shit just got real.

I want evidence that there is, indeed, a time when the Verizon store isn't crowded. I try to avoid this place, but sometimes you just have to enter its unnerving clutch. And every single time, there are people lounging and waiting; browsing and waiting; getting irritated and cursing, but still waiting. We walk in and I give the guy with the tablet my name and he tells me it should be about thirty minutes, which really means an eternity.

So we browse, checking out phones and cases. Beth tells me I should have asked for more money because she wants this adorable Hello Kitty case for her phone. Charlie tells me I should pick up the home security kit, see if Officer Howard will install it. Fortunately, he didn't follow us into the store, but he's visible through the floor-to-ceiling windows, sitting in the sun like a lizard—completely still.

"Avery? Avery Chase?" the guy with the tablet calls, twenty-eight minutes later. I roll up and he hands me off to some guy named Doug, who looks at me, tilts his head, but goes no further with what he's thinking. I tense, but then try to relax, give him the benefit of the doubt.

"So what are we doing today?" Doug asks.

I take out my broken phone. "Replacing this."

"Whoa! That's totally wrecked. What happened?"

Somehow I'm not prepared to tell him the truth, nor am I prepared to lie. Beth has no problem, though.

"I accidentally stepped on it," she says and Doug nods. "While it was in his pocket."

Doug is confused, but lets it go and looks up my family's account. He then looks up at me again, and this time the recognition is clear. "You're Avery Chase."

I don't reply. I know exactly where this is going.

"As in like the transgender kid. I've heard about you." Doug smiles at his recognition, like he's spotted the Abominable Snowman or some shit. Beth and Charlie, however, have crept protectively closer.

"Wow, look at me. Sorry. I've just heard about you and all, and I think what you're doing is great. Brave."

"Thanks." I hope the one word can end this now.

"Oh, you're welcome. I mean it's just so crazy. You, legit, look like a guy." He leans closer.

This is why my life is so fucked up. Not just because of how I feel but because of how douches like this get to exist and try to pry into it.

"The phone, Doug. Focus on the phone," Beth says, and her tone means business.

He looks at her. Really looks at her. And then I watch his focus shift to Charlie. "Right. So which one of you is with who? Or are you like all trannies?"

I'm tiny by male standards, but Doug is more soft than I am small. So when I run at him, putting my head into his chest, he goes down like an enormous water balloon. His body *thwacks* with a density that makes me smile. He rolls onto his back and holds his head.

This brings Officer Howard out of his mannequin pose and into the store faster than I thought possible. His entrance ushers in an unnatural silence for an electronics store, and we all silently watch as Doug is helped to his feet by a manager who has no clue who to speak to first. Fortunately, my shadow knows how to do his job.

"I'm going to need you to wrap this up as soon as possible. This is official police business."

The manager looks at us and then Doug. "Go in the back and take a break. We'll talk later."

Doug shuffles on and the manager looks at me and my busted phone. "How can I help you, sir?"

"Let's start with my phone, but I've got my eye on this case that I think you should also throw in."

"Certainly," the manager says.

Almost an hour later I'm good to go. I hand over my broken phone to Officer Howard and the manager watches this, pensively. Doug has yet to reemerge. Which is good, because now that I'm calm, I may just chew his ass out instead of putting him on it.

We go to leave but Charlie stops us. "Check it," he says.

On the television above him the press conference Tom promised is getting underway. Officer Howard turns back to the manager. "Turn off the music."

A moment later the background noise is gone, and all that is audible is the television and the whispers of the customers, now gathered around it.

Tom's boss, Captain James, stands behind a podium, which appears to be in the vestibule of the police station. He's flanked by a number of officers, but not Tom. He adjusts the mic and then looks out into the room of reporters.

"As you are all well aware, we have recently been investigating the disappearance and death of Mary Matthison. It is an ongoing investigation, but I felt it time to bring the community up to speed as best I can without compromising the integrity of the case."

My binder is meant to constrict, meant to pull my breasts flat. I'm used to the way it can leave me slightly breathless. But what I feel now, listening to the captain, is as if a corset has been slipped into my binder's place, and someone is tightening it while their foot is lodged into my back.

"We can say with confidence that Mary Matthison was murdered. All evidence suggests that it was a violent encounter with a perpetrator that should be considered extremely dangerous." The captain pauses, looks over the room, and it feels as if he's looking out, past the reporters, past the walls of the station, and to us, hoping he'll catch sight of the murderer watching his game play out.

"And to that end, we feel it necessary to warn you. Let there be no gray area on this: there's a killer among us."

Hands shoot up, cameras flash, but the captain ignores it.

"Evidence has been uncovered today that is helping us narrow down our list of suspects. Because we do have a list. It is our greatest hope that we can bring the killer to justice and bring closure to the Matthison family, who has served our community for decades."

My insides roil with emotions, each wrestling the other for dominance. But none wins as the captain closes out his speech.

"Tomorrow we bury Mary Matthison. Our high school will be closed so her peers may attend. I urge you parents to talk to your children, ask them what they know. And then hold them tight. In my tenure as an officer and now a captain, nothing enrages me like the death of a child. We will not rest until justice has been served."

The conference ends and yet I stare at the television, wishing the captain would return and speak more. Because now that he's gone, I'm back here in some stupid store with stupid bigoted people. For a moment I was transported into the fight, into the good of what I know of police work and of forensics.

There is truth to be found. But seeking it, and then finding it, first take knowing where to look.

CHAPTER 8

My alarm clock goes off at the regular time, hours before I need it to, but I don't want to rush this morning. I need as much time as I can gather to prepare for Mary's funeral.

I stand and stretch but there's no point in turning on the TV or going online. If anything had broken in the case, I'd already know. I peer out my window at the cruiser parked there. Whoever's on duty is drinking coffee and watching the street.

Last night was rough, period. As soon as I got home my parents were all over me, wanting to know why I hadn't told them anything, shown them the texts, etcetera. Tom told them, and I don't blame him for doing that. Keeping me safe has always been a top priority for him.

"Remember those death threats back in eighth grade?" I asked. Of course they remembered. I don't think they will ever forget having to take me out of school and going straight to the police, and then the doctor's. "Well, remember how they never really figured out who it was?"

My parents waited for me to answer my own question.

"Well, it's the same thing, I guess. But this time I wanted to know before I said anything. Because if the threats were real and Tom could connect the dots, it would solve the case."

"Avery," Mom said, and grabbed me for a hug. "You cannot risk your life like that. You can't sacrifice yourself in order to solve the case." She paused but I knew what was coming. "Mary would never want that."

"I know, but what am I supposed to do? Hide until they've caught Mary's killer? What if they never do? I'd blame myself, you know that. I'd blame myself and I know I couldn't recover from that. So it's better for me to be where I am."

"As a target?" Tyler, who'd walked into the room, asked.

"Yeah. It's not like that's something new for me."

He thought about this and then went to the bay window at the front of the house. "But this guy is." We all looked at the cruiser and my new best friend.

Tyler and Dad's conversation out in the hall pulls me out of yesterday.

"It's up to you, bud. Your school is open, but you don't have to go. We'll write you a note." Dad's voice carries through my door, but Tyler's answer is muffled.

I open and look out. "Hey, what's up?"

Dad starts answering, but Tyler sees me and makes a beeline to my room. I step out of the way, and he plops on my bed. Dad gives me a look but then waves me off. I close the door.

"So, what's the deal, school or no school?"

He rolls over. "I don't know."

"Really?" I think about this for a second. "Well, I guess I take that back. Both are pretty shitty options."

"Exactly," he says. "I'd rather just stay home."

"Same here."

He sits up. "You okay?"

I'm struck, because Tyler doesn't ask this. He's thirteen. All that exists to him are his friends, school, and himself. I don't blame him for that, either. He puts up with a ton because of me. Someday I'll make it up to him. I just don't know how.

"No, little man. Not even close." I shake my head. "But what about you? Something up at school, because I know you don't hate it that much."

He looks down at his lap. "Everyone's all been, 'You gotta go. It's the right thing to do.' But those kids just want to get out of class for a day. They don't really care about Mary."

My heart thumps an extra beat. He's a good kid. "What about you?"

Tyler looks out my window. "Av, I'm sorry, but, like, I know the two of you were close, and I'm sad for you. I feel terrible for her parents." He pauses. "But I only have some memories of Mary. I remember her being awesome. But *I'm* not really sad." He looks at me. "Does that make me a bad person?"

A crack opens in my chest, and I sit on the bed with him. "Not at all. You have more intelligence than half my school."

He laughs.

"It's the same thing there, people are happy to have the day off, and some are talking about Mary's funeral as if they're going to see a show. It's sick, but what can you do? People are awful sometimes."

"Yeah, they are." There's something about how he says this, the authority with which he speaks, that's unnerving.

"Something happen?"

"Smack talk about you, stupid questions. The case, you know, people are talking about Mary, and you came up."

I am ashamed of myself for putting him through this. "Anything in particular? Any of those questions you need me to answer? I can help."

Tyler rubs his face, hesitates, and then says, "You don't have a penis, right?"

I crack up and he looks upset, so I rub the top of his head. "No, Ty. I don't. Taking testosterone doesn't grow one for you. If it did all the boys in your school would be robbing pharmacies."

He thinks this over for a second and then laughs hard, his voice going deep as he does. He's changing, and this is only going to get more difficult. But I know it will get better.

"So you want out of this, some time to yourself?" I ask.

"Is that bad?"

"Not at all. No one who cares about you thinks otherwise. Okay?"

"Yeah. Thanks, Av."

"No problem. Now, here's what we'll do, you promise Dad that when he gets home from the funeral, you'll rake the rest of the leaves. You lay low until then and if anyone asks, we can just make up some excuse like you had diarrhea or something. Trust me, once you mention bodily fluids, people don't want to hear any more. Cool?"

Tyler hops off the bed. "That is awesome."

"That is *not* awesome," Dad says through the door. "But it's fine. You stay here, and then it's yard work for the both of us for the afternoon."

Tyler runs to the door and wrenches it open. He puts out his hand. "Deal."

Dad peers in at me and then shakes my brother's hand. "Deal."

Tyler takes off down the hall and Mom appears. "What's going on?"

"I'd like to get ready if that's all right," I say, my hand on the doorknob.

"Gotcha," Dad says. "Thanks."

It was only a year ago that my grandfather died and Dad brought me to get a suit. The tailor was this old guy who could tell my proportions were off, but didn't seem to understand why. He mumbled something about "curves" but that was it. Dad made him leave things a bit long, which I didn't understand. I had to roll the pants and sleeves.

But now that I slide the pants on, I get it. I grew. The pants are perfect. And so is the jacket, even with my binder. This shouldn't make me emotional, but I feel like running out and hugging my father right now. But I don't. I find my black tie and shoes and toss them on my bed.

I sit next to them and put my head in my hands. I know with as much certainty that I loved Mary, that I will cry a river of tears today. I hope they come later, when I'm alone, and don't have to face anyone. But I can feel them lurking just behind my eyes. My throat is already tightening, and I see her, and her fear. I hear her scream and watch her run. And I join in. Because the reverend is at our backs.

Beth climbs in, gorgeous in her black dress and shawl, laces her fingers into mine, and then kisses me on the lips. She pulls back. "How you holding up?"

"Minute by minute." I lift up her hand and kiss it. "Thanks."

"I see we've got company." Beth looks into the rearview mirror at the shadow following.

"I thought I would hate it, but I really don't mind." I pull away, headed toward Charlie's.

"Nothing new? No messages last night?"

"I would have called you, trust me. I know it was stupid the first time to just let it go."

"Not stupid. You're scared. We all are. And being scared makes it hard to think."

Except I can't seem to turn off my brain. Thinking is all I do. But Beth is right. Nothing that kept me awake last night staring at the ceiling has brought me any clarity.

"I wish I knew her more. We really never had much interaction. You know?"

Of course I know. You don't get a Beth from an ultrareligious family. Her parents are awesome and supportive and I feel so comfortable around them. Yet Mary's emotions weren't so different than Beth's. So maybe I'm wrong. Maybe it's not the religion, but the home. The environment. Mary was like her mom in so many ways: sweet, compassionate, and smart.

"I wish you did, too, but if that were the case, who knows, maybe you would have gone after her and not me."

Beth smiles. "Having an open mind does make life more interesting."

We pull up to Charlie's and he walks out the door, looking natural in his charcoal suit, as if he wears it every week. He says, "Hey," when he gets in, nothing more. I wonder what this must be doing to him, what his memories must be. I don't want to lift that scab more than he already is, so I don't say a word about his mother.

A few minutes later, we arrive, and finding a place to park is a near impossibility. It's like we're headed to a concert and not the saddest day of my entire life.

After I park, we step out and into a wall of noise. Rumors, everywhere. As we walk, I eavesdrop and am torn. Part of me wants everyone to shut up and pay some respect, but another part is thrilled to see the turnout. They may be here because of the nature of Mary's death and the scene it's created, but I also think a lot are here because of how she lived, who she was. That's a testament.

I spy Tom among his men, directing traffic and keeping the reporters at a distance. He nods to me and I wave back. Then we head inside, and the noise in here is the same as outside.

We sit in the middle, closer to the back than front, and don't speak. Beth takes my hand. I watch Charlie swallow and close his eyes.

Up from us, the flock has taken two rows. They are silent, staring forward at the cross. Their devoutness is stunning. Amid a church that is nonstop chatter, they focus on what must be getting them through this. Because like them or not, they were still Mary's friends, and so this has to hurt. Possibly as much as my own pain.

Bagpipes kick in with "Amazing Grace" and my insides feel as if they're being pulled straight through my chest.

We stand and the pallbearers come up the aisle, all in black, except for their white gloves. Calder is on the right, and his eyes are dead, staring straight ahead as if he's on a hike through a nightmare. But he and the others are stoic, severe, and dry-eyed. They are the only ones who seem to be, though.

The music hushed the talking and now seems to have exposed the truth of the moment, and people are responding as they should.

As the pallbearers make their way up the aisle shouldering the casket shrouded in the church cloth, sobs echo off the marble of the altar.

I close my eyes and I see Mary's smiling face, some scene from when everything was simple, if that was ever true. When I open them, tears cloud her passing.

We all turn and watch a guest reverend greet her casket, say a few words to the pallbearers and to the family, and then begin his service.

I wonder why Matthison turned over the reins. But then I see him with his wife and how she hangs on him. It was the right move. And because I don't care for the service, the religion that hates me, I tune out. I stand when I'm supposed to, and sit and kneel and mouth the words when we sing. But I can't focus on what the reverend has to say. My mind is filled with too many memories, too many emotions. It is a swirl of echoes from the present and past.

Then the room stirs, followed by an audible silence, and I come around. Reverend Matthison rises, kisses his wife, and takes his place behind the podium. His podium. The microphone pops and crackles as he positions it. We wait.

He pulls a paper from his suit and then looks at us for the briefest of moments. I cannot read his face, cannot imagine what he's thinking. Then he begins.

"Mary was a good girl. She was compassionate and generous to a fault." He pauses, either to collect himself, or to let that idea sink in. "There isn't a person in this room that can speak ill of our daughter. That is not a boast from a proud parent, but a fact that I am proud to claim. But it is not my doing. It was Mary's. She was better than I have ever been, and I am proud to have raised a daughter of such grace."

Matthison pauses again, and I look around. Everyone is hanging on to his every word. I think of something I said to Charlie: *everyone has enemies.* In spite of what Matthison's saying, Mary did, too, or we wouldn't be here. And I know he's in pain, and that this is a holy place, *his* sanctuary, but in his eyes, I don't see only pain. There's more. It's like I'm looking inside him. Like he's baring his soul. And it's not as pure as I expected it to be.

"I do not know why she has been taken. I do not pretend to understand how the world works, but I do know that we should remember the words from Galatians: 'Be not deceived; God is not mocked: for whatsoever a man soweth, that shall he also reap.'" Matthison lets this one hang in the air for a moment. I shift uncomfortably.

"This is God's plan. And so we must accept it, and move on." He looks directly at his daughter's casket. "Only I have no idea how." He returns to us. "So I will follow in Mary's footsteps. I will let her lead. I will serve her by honoring all she stood for, all she was." Reverend Matthison clears his throat. "I suggest that if you feel as lost as I do, you do the same. Let Mary be a beacon in this darkest of hours."

As he moves away from the podium, the echoes of his words die away, but reverberate within me. Mary was a wonderful person. I loved her. Still love her. The reverend's right. She will lead, and I will follow, wherever that takes me, however much darkness I need to go through in order to find her light.

The ride to the cemetery is quiet. No one speaks because there is nothing worth saying.

We stop with the remainder of the cars as they navigate into the narrow opening. Most of what seems like a half-mile train of vehicles will have to park on the road and walk in. But there's a police escort, as well as officers inside the cemetery. The media's been isolated to a section across the street. I don't see Tom, but I'm sure he's lurking somewhere.

We park and make our way to Mary's grave.

I know the AstroTurf is supposed to make the open ground look a little less ominous, but it strikes me as such a pathetic decoy as we stand across from the Matthisons, seated beneath a pop-up tent, all holding yellow roses. Mrs. Matthison hasn't once looked up from the casket, and clings to her husband for support. I hope she's medicated. It's only fair.

The reverend from the church waits until all have arrived, a group so enormous the remainder of the cemetery is obscured. It's just a sea of black against the falling leaves.

The guest reverend reads from the Bible, says a few words that are no match for the power of the eulogy, and then directs the pallbearers to say their last good-byes and leave their gloves on the casket along with the flowers they have been given. They do as told, and I hold a breath as Calder approaches. He stares at Mary's casket, still looking very much like he's in some dream he cannot wake from. His mouth moves, in prayer, some last "I love you," I can't tell. But he moves back and joins the rest of the men, and they pull him into an embrace as he openly wails.

I have to turn away, the pain is so intense. This moment is pure torture, which I wish was both over, and in a weird way, would never end. Because we get to leave; Mary stays.

The family rises and does the same as the pallbearers, and there isn't a dry eye. Some squeeze the shoulders of Mary's parents, and others, just slip behind a nearby tombstone, backs racking with sobs. The flock moves as a knot, and I'm not surprised to see them stop and hold Calder, especially Eva.

Mary's parents go to the casket last, and it takes a good deal of urging to get Mary's mother to stand, but Reverend Matthison manages to do so, and then he places a flower, says some words, kisses his fingertips and touches them to the casket. With much coaxing, Mrs. Matthison does the same, and then they embrace and hold each other so tight, it's breathtaking.

The guest reverend then motions for us to take a flower from the arrangements strewn next to the grave. Slowly, people make their way forward and we join them. I hold Beth's hand and I look over at Charlie. He must sense I'm watching because he looks up. His eyes are as filled as mine, and he nods, causing the tears to drop onto his cheeks. And in this silent exchange is everything.

The line moves and people have their moment. I see my parents up ahead. They pause and hold on to each other and say their good-byes. They loved her, too. I have no doubt about that.

The sky is clear and blue and beautiful, and I am holding the hand of my girlfriend, feeling as if my soul has been wrenched from me. I think I understand the word "gutted" now. For all that I have changed, so much has remained the same. I still love her. And I whisper this as I drop my flower.

Beth and I move away from the grave and as soon as we're past the crowd I turn to her. I just want to be held. I feel so utterly lost, so deeply hurt that I could sit down and not move for the rest of the day.

After a while people begin to clear out, and I see my parents making small talk under a tree. I look for Charlie, to ask if he's ready to go, but when I do, he's not with us. Beth guides my head. "Over there."

In the distance, Charlie stands before his mom's grave. His head's tilted to the side as if listening to her. And maybe he is.

I leave Beth and go to him. He sees me and looks up, wipes his eyes. "Hey, Av."

At his side, we stare at the headstone and I ask if he's okay.

"No, man, not even remotely. I'm sad and angry and depressed all at the same time." He clears his throat. "But I'm hopeful, too."

I turn to him. "Why's that?"

"You saw him, right? How dead he looked. That's guilt. It's eating him from the inside out."

I think I know who he means, but I'm taking nothing for granted today. "Calder or Matthison?"

"Calder. He's a zombie. I can't believe it was the reverend. That would mean he killed his own daughter and left her in the woods. There's no way. Not after that eulogy he gave."

I don't want to argue with Charlie, especially not now, at the end of Mary's service, while we're standing at his mother's headstone, but I disagree with him. All these memories that have surfaced have brought up ones I've tucked away in some effort to protect myself. Maybe they're distorted, or maybe they're exactly as things were. All I know is that when I think about that day with Mary, I can't help remembering what happened after, with her father. And when I saw his eyes today, they brought me even further back, into the crevices and the darkness in which I know Mary lived. Maybe this is where my loathing for the flock comes from, even more than their hatred of who I am. I can't be sure. I can't be sure of anything in this moment.

I squeeze Charlie's shoulder and he leans against me.

I touch his mom's headstone. "She's proud of you, Charlie. I know it. Whether you and I figure this out or the cops do. She still loves you."

He collapses into me, and I hold him until he's able to see again.

There is no formal gathering after the service. The sheer number of people precludes it. So groups head in separate directions, and I wonder how many will actually spend time thinking of Mary and how many will spend it as just another day off.

My parents come over to Beth, Charlie, and me. They give hugs all around. "I'm off to that yard work," Dad says.

"I planned to go into work, but if you need me at home, I'm there."

I love that Mom offered, but I don't want to be with either of them right now. Beth and Charlie are who I need.

"No, I'm good," I say. "We're just going to get something to eat." I turn to Dad. "Maybe I'll help you and Tyler later."

"Don't rush on our behalf," he says, and then they're gone.

"Your parents kind of kick ass, Avery," Beth says.

"Agreed." Charlie nods as he watches them go.

"I'm not going to argue with you, but isn't their job to be awesome? Like all parents, that's the point, right?"

We start walking, some of the last to remain. "Sure," Beth says, "but that's easier said than done, I think."

"Don't feed this troll," Charlie says. "He's still convinced that Matthison's a suspect."

"Really?" Beth whips toward me. "Your ears work,

right? So you heard what he said about Mary. That guy loves her."

"I heard. And I'm not saying he didn't love her. I just think there's more to it."

"The religion?" Charlie asks.

Our footsteps crunch through the gravel and I see my car, and my bodyguard up ahead. "Maybe." I stop walking. "Thing is, I was around their house as a kid, mostly hiding from the reverend, so I think I heard and saw things others didn't. The reverend's got a temper. And that whole 'spare the rod, spoil the child' thing isn't just something they said."

"Are you telling us that Matthison beat Mary?"

I nod, but quickly clarify. "He hit her, yeah. *Beat* is a bit much, but really, anytime you hit your kid, it's fucked up."

"You saw this? You saw him hit her?" Charlie asks.

"Yeah, and the bruises after."

Beth and Charlie turn away from me, absorbing what I've said. "Why?" Beth asks. "What'd she do?"

I think of that day and of how to answer, how to encapsulate all that transpired so that it makes sense. But it still doesn't make any sense to me. My phone chimes with a text, though, so for the moment I don't have to.

My heart stops when I look at the screen. It's a different number from before, but the messenger seems to be the same: *I wanted to give you a chance to mourn before I showed you some things.*

"Hey," I say, and wave them to me. Beth and Charlie read over my shoulders, and we watch the next text forming.

I'm not sure you understood what I want, so let me help you.

"Av, what is going on?" Charlie asks.

I wish I knew.

A new text emerges, with a picture attached. The picture is of me when I was young, still very much looking like a little girl, pigtails and all. The text says: *This! This is who you are! Until I see you as you should be, this is possible . . .*

The image bothers me and the text itself is shocking, but what I'm truly afraid of is the ellipsis, those three little dots. Because I don't know what's coming, what's next.

I drop my phone when I have the answer. No amount of time studying forensics, staring at images from the Body Farm in Quantico, has prepared me for what is lying at my feet on my phone.

Charlie picks it up, I think because he didn't see. Because when he looks he yells, "What the fuck?"

Beth holds me tight, but leans across to see. "Jesus!" she screams and tucks her face into my chest.

I look at Charlie and his eyes are wild. He shakes his head. "Is that? Is that her?"

I nod.

"How do you know?"

It's the message, not the other part, the missing pieces, that make me certain. The picture is of Mary, dead in the woods, her body on the ground, surrounded by wet leaves. Her mouth is wrenched open, and the paper inside pokes out like a white tongue. Her eyes have been removed, gouged out it seems, and the black voids staring back are merciless.

I feel like I might hurl, or pass out, or both at the same time. My phone chimes again.

It's in Charlie's hands and he looks at me like he's about to have a panic attack. "No, Av, there can't be more."

But I remember what those cops said. Something has been done to her body. *This* must be it. But why show them to me? Is this really the threat? That this will also be done to me if I don't what, dress more like a girl? It makes no sense. But I'm behaving as if a murderer is operating on logic, and has a heart.

I take the phone from Charlie and I breathe deep. I have to see what I don't want to see. I turn my phone over and stare at the screen.

It's another image of Mary. Another one from the crime scene. Thankfully, it is not of her face, which allows me to take in this picture more than the other. But I'm confused. It's a shot of the back of her head, her hair pulled up into a high ponytail. I almost ask Beth and Charlie to look, to help me understand, but then I see it, what has been done, and I can't unsee it.

Her ears have been removed, cut clean from the side of her face, leaving nothing but the twisting canals beneath.

Before I can process, before I can make any sense of what the hell is going on, another text comes, this one shooting out in a green bubble. Words only. Just words: *See no evil, hear no evil . . .*

"Speak no evil," I say aloud and Charlie and Beth turn to me.

"He also cut her ears off," I say. "And then he sent the message, see no evil . . ."

Charlie finishes for me. "Hear no evil, speak no evil." He looks out over the horizon. "He's taken pieces of her." There's a pause, then he says, "Go back to that first pic, Av."

"What? I don't want to look at that again."

"You have to."

I scroll up to the text, hit the image, and then the awful picture sits before us. Charlie and I see it at the same time, the last piece of the puzzle we somehow missed because of the heinousness of the first. Not only have Mary's eyes been removed, but her mouth isn't wide open, it just appears that way. It's cracked only a bit, as if she's mildly surprised. It's the extensive amount of teeth that throws off the arrangement. Her lips have been removed.

Beth looks on with us and then leans against a nearby tree and vomits. Her puke hits the roots and splatters over her beautiful shoes. I rub her back and wait.

Nothing else comes, not an image, not a text, and no more hurl.

We stand, silent, confused, and I realize at the trembling of my legs, terrified.

I call Tom.

"Avery? What's up?"

"Where are you?" I hear my words as they are spilling out of my mouth. They're not firm consonants and vowels.

"Are you okay? Did something happen? Have you been in an accident?"

I wish I could say yes. It feels like I have been. But nothing about this is accidental. This isn't some little prank by an ignorant eighth grader. This is intentional malice. This is murder and mutilation.

"He sent me pictures of her, Tom."

There's a pause. "What do you mean?"

"Mary. He took out her eyes? He cut off her ears?" I sputter. "He . . . he took her mouth, too?"

"Avery, how do you know this?" Tom asks and I hear the sounds of him getting into a car in the background.

"I just told you!" I don't mean to yell, but I can't help it.

"I know, I know. It's just," and Tom pauses again. I hear his siren blaring. "Avery, we've only recovered her eyes. That's what we found at the Matthison's, yesterday."

My body locks up, thoroughly frozen. "So . . ." I can't finish.

"So, Officer Howard is coming to you. He will not leave your side until I get there. Now, tell me, did he say anything? Did he text you as well as send pictures?"

Officer Howard is visible now, running toward us, his gun in hand. This image is supposed to make me feel safe, but I'm so numb, I can't tell if that's true.

"Yes."

"Okay? What? What was the message?"

"He's going to kill me, Tom."

Beth and Charlie turn away from the confusion of the approaching, gun-wielding officer and look at me. That what I'm saying is more alarming speaks volumes.

"What? He wrote that? Again?"

"No. He threatened me. He told me to repent. To dress like a girl. Or to be a girl, I don't know."

"Shit," Tom says.

"I won't do it," I say, with a conviction that makes no sense in this moment. "I'm not a fucking girl! Do you hear me? I'm not a girl! I. AM. NOT. A. GIRL!"

The cemetery echoes with my words. If Tom replies I don't hear him, because my phone chimes again. Another text.

Yes, you are.

Home. I know we got here in the back of Tom's cruiser, but little else has processed aside from that text exchange.

Officer Howard comes out my front door and then speaks through Tom's open window. "All clear."

Tom lets us out of the car. Ty and Dad are waiting for us on the front lawn.

"Tom, okay, now can you tell me what's going on?" Dad asks.

"Once we're inside. I promise."

One officer stays stationed at our front door. Another heads to the back.

Another three officers, Tom, and the captain, follow us in. We head straight for the living room and collapse onto the couches.

Beth stares at the TV, but it's not on. Charlie keeps looking out the window or up at the ceiling. He's thinking, probably has a thousand ideas, already.

I'm petrified. Not that I'll say it, but the fact that I know the killer is watching me stops my heart. He could be watching me right now. How? And for how long? And, of course, why? Why would he do this to Mary? How does that have anything to do with me? Could I really be next?

Beth squeezes my hand. "Are you all right?" she asks.

"No." I keep seeing those pictures. I'm sure we all are. "You?"

"I've never been so scared, Avery."

The officers stay standing, as do Dad and Tom, but Captain James sits on the edge of the couch across from the three of us. He looks much more average than yesterday, sitting with us, rather than standing behind a podium. Or is it how less sure of himself he seems? Yesterday he had an air of confidence. Now, he looks defeated.

"Avery, I'm going to be direct with you, because time is of the essence. I'm sorry if this seems insensitive."

"I understand," I say, even though I don't, not about anything.

Captain James nods. "We've reviewed the photos sent, and while I cannot speak to the authenticity, I will say they are quite disturbing. Unfortunately, we could not pinpoint the phones those texts have come from. Both used a cell tower here in town, but that's as far as the trail goes."

In spite of this fog I'm in, I listen to the captain's words and watch him as he unfolds what he knows, while hoping to see what he's withholding. But he's got a true poker face.

"At this point, Avery, we are very concerned about your safety. We are treating this as a legitimate threat by the person who killed Mary Matthison. Those images you received leave us no other choice."

In spite of knowing this to be the only plausible outcome, it's shocking as hell to hear these words from the captain. Ever since I declared who I am, I've worn a target. And now that target has made me a potential murder victim. Just like Mary.

"How do I connect to what happened to Mary?" I ask and am surprised at how low and calm my voice is. It's little solace, however.

"That is our question to you, Avery. And to any of you." The captain opens his arms to indicate the rest of us on the couch. "Could you explain your relationship with Mary? Can you shed any light on how her death and threat against your life might intersect?"

Of course I can. I could tell story after story of how Mary stood up for me, time and time again at school. I could talk about our friendship and whatever else it was we had. I could explain how badly that ended because of the reverend. Really, how futile all of her attempts were to protect me. The town's sense of who I am, its religion, and how I can't possibly be me, there's the *intersection*.

I could explain how because of that Mary then turned from me, stupidly, into the devout embrace of Calder, who, in spite of currently looking like the walking dead, is one of the most pious, self-righteous assholes I know. He's a miniature Reverend Matthison in the making, and so it's no great leap to understand why Mary felt something toward him. What is, however, is that the overwhelming response wasn't revulsion. Which is probably why they fought. They had sex, and it opened her eyes. Mistakes tend to do that.

But I can't say any of these things. No one saw what I saw. No one else was as close but in the shadows. This town loves Reverend Matthison and his daughter. Who am I, Avery *fucking* Chase, weird-ass, freak, to slander the name? Or is this how I get through the dark? If I speak, am I doing what Mary would have wanted?

I look up to answer, to say what, I don't know. But then I see him, the asshole from the woods, Officer Wright. I don't know how I missed him before, but he sees me, and there's a smirk there, and I remember him, not only from the woods, but from Mary's house. He's part of the congregation. He used to come by, pay a visit. He's older now and has a mustache, but his eyes, they haven't changed. That same unnerving way they had of looking through me then, they still have now.

"Sure," I say, finally answering the captain. "Get rid of him, first." I point directly at Wright.

He seems offended as all eyes turn to him.

"What's the matter with Officer Wright?" the captain asks, turning back to me.

I keep my eyes on the cop when I answer. "Ask him about our time together in the woods."

Maybe it's the wording I chose or the tone of my voice, but Beth grabs my hand, and not in a pleasant way.

Officer Wright frowns, then answers. "Captain, you know about Avery's incident in the woods. I am the one who apprehended him."

The captain nods. "Okay. So what's the problem, Avery?"

There's an entire room of men looking at me, looking for me to answer this question, including my father. My girlfriend, best friend, and younger brother are seated on the couch with me. I'm being interrogated in my own house. And now I'm pissed, but when I open my mouth to tell the captain off for not knowing, that answer doesn't emerge.

"He's a bigot, Captain."

"Excuse me?"

"That day in the woods, he questioned me. He called me a freak, wanted to say more, I could tell. He hates who I am because his religion tells him to. Do you really think I want to help you if he's in the mix?"

There's a whole lot of uncomfortable shuffling around the room, and then Captain James holds up his hands. I sneak a look at Officer Wright and he looks ready to implode. "Hold on, Avery, hold on. I'm sorry if Officer Wright was a little rough, but I'm sure you can understand that he was doing his job under a tense situation. I'm positive nothing was intended. . . ."

"Don't talk to me like I'm a child, as if this is the first time someone's treated me this way, and that I don't know what was going on," I say, cutting off Captain James. "You have no idea how it is to be in my shoes, what I have to deal with. And so when I tell you one of your men, just one—I'm not calling out the entire squad. When I say he's a bigot, trust that what I'm saying comes from a place of truth. If you can't do that, then I have nothing else to say to you."

The room is so quiet and so tense it's painful to experience. I keep my eyes trained on Captain James and his poker face. "Okay, I understand," he says. "I will personally deal with this matter. But right now I need answers from you about this case."

I lean forward now and try to look as pissed as I feel. "Then get him the fuck out of this room."

The air explodes with screaming and threats and accusations. The officers won't stand for this. I sit back and watch it all. Dad pushes his way through and stands in front of me. "What can I do?" he asks.

"Clear the room. No one stays but Tom."

Dad, who works from home and who enjoys cooking and baking, turns to a roomful of men who investigate crimes on a daily basis. He's as equipped to make this demand as I am to ask him to do it.

"Out! All of you, out!"

They look at him, stunned silent.

"You heard me. Everyone but Tom. Go! Now!"

Captain James starts to protest. Dad, like me, cuts him off.

"I understand. You're trying to help. But you're failing. We'll talk to my brother. You need anything else, we'll just have to see."

The captain stands in a huff, and he marches out with his men.

When the front door closes behind the last officer, Tom leans his forehead against it. "Avery? What the hell?" Tom says, head still against the door.

"You don't understand," I say. "That guy, he's twisted."

Tom steps away enough to rub his face. "Yeah, I do. But that doesn't change the case, or change the fact that you're in danger." He turns and faces me now. "Why didn't you just answer his question?"

"Because it's more complicated than it seems," I say.

"Well, help me, bud. Uncomplicate it. Or leave it complicated, but give me the details. If I walk out of here with nothing, I'm done."

"Tom, now's not the time to be dramatic," Dad says, and Tom wheels on him.

"Gordon, I'm not being *dramatic*. I'm sorry you don't get this. There's a dead girl and your son could be next if we don't understand the connection. If I walk out of here with a big handful of nothing, the captain will have my ass."

"So it's *your job* you care about then?"

"No, goddamnit! I care about my nephew. I care about this town. I care about Mary. I want to catch this killer. So I need Avery to stop hiding and to open up."

"Do you have any idea how hard that is for him to do?" Dad's in his face now. I love him for this.

"I do." Tom's voice has dropped. "I really do. And I promise to keep him safe." He looks at me. "Do you trust me, Av?"

I do. Tom has pulled me out of more shit than anyone else in my family. He truly has gone the extra mile, more than has ever been necessary. So, as difficult as this is going to be, I'll show him what he's never seen.

"Dad, can you drive Beth and Charlie home?"

All three look at me and Beth says, "I'm staying."

I turn to her. "You can't. It has to be Tom. Just Tom." I look at Charlie. "I'll call you later."

"Your phone will be tapped, but that's cool." He stands. "Come on, Beth." He extends his hand for her, but she doesn't take it. She moves away from me and then stands quickly. She doesn't look back as she goes through the door.

"It'll be all right," Charlie says. "Come on, Tyler."

Dad turns to my brother. "Good idea." Then he goes to the wall and grabs his keys. When he comes back down the hallway, Tom stops him.

"Thanks, Gord."

"Don't thank me. Just catch this sonofabitch."

They leave, and even though I asked for this, I'm so uncomfortable having this conversation I want to ask Tom to join everyone else. I want to tell him I'll write it down. Because saying it, especially face-to-face, feels like confession. And I don't need any more judgment in my life.

"It's okay, Avery. I'll only give them the details that are pertinent. I can paint a picture without every brushstroke."

I look at the floor. I hear him, but I see Mary. Our past. The last day we ever had together. The same day we were in the swimming hole down from her house. It all comes back, as memory does, in trickles, and then a flood.

His eyes lock on us and then he screams. "Mary Grace, what are you doing?" The noise echoes deep into the woods and I shake. She ignores her father, grabs my face, and looks in my eyes. She's afraid, but calm.

"Run. We have to run."

Neither of us has shoes, but we take off. The pine needles soften the ground, but branches crack beneath our feet, and I feel the dull throb of striking stones. But Mary forges ahead because of the lumbering noise behind us, Reverend Matthison at full speed.

She jumps a fallen log and we scramble down a hill. I have no spare breath to ask where we are going, so I just follow and hope we get away. Mary looks back and waves her hand over her shoulder, directing. But I see nothing but trees, feel nothing but searing pain in my feet, the dampness of my clothes sticking, and the heat of the day, as oppressive as the sound of her father, fifty yards behind.

There's a break in the floor of the woods, larger rocks opening up a trickle of a stream, and Mary vaults over and clings to a cluster of large, moss-covered stones. She scrabbles, hand-over-hand across them and then disappears. I stop, confused, but then see her arm extend from within them, beckoning to me.

I follow, and in a moment, squeeze through the small opening. We are inside the stone formation. It's like a hollowed-out tree. Light enters in shafts that illuminate enough for the water beneath to be visible, to see where Mary sits on a rock, holding her knees to her chest.

"Mary! Mary where are you?" Reverend Matthison's voice booms within our space, as if he's inside. But his footsteps crack outside our barrier, and in a minute he moves away.

"What the . . ."

Mary puts a hand over my mouth and shakes her head, the point obvious. I nod and she takes it away. Her eyes are frenzied, but she takes a deep breath, unfurls her legs, and puts her feet in the water. Hers are as cut up as mine, and so I do the same. The water is colder than in the swimming hole and feels glorious on my screaming feet. I look around and wonder how many times she's been here. Mary's never mentioned it before, but maybe that's because it was too much. Like today. And whatever lies ahead.

She looks at me, sun casting a band of light across her eyes. I reach out and grab her hand. She squeezes tight, and we sit, waiting for the danger to pass.

I wish a shower could wash away the inside as well as the outside. I would stand underneath this nozzle all day, letting the water pour over and through me if it meant I'd feel clean, feel like myself once I got out, had managed to scour out all that terrifies me, both the old and everything connected to Mary's death.

But that's an impossibility, because last night's conversation with Tom has yet to leave my head. Certain questions won't quit.

"So the reverend was rough with Mary?"

I told Tom what I'd seen. It was enough.

"What about Calder? The same as the reverend?"

Calder and Mary never made any sense to me. She was open-minded and gentle and sweet. Calder is a tool. To him, Bible passages are more important than mathematical equations or science. He's cocky and arrogant, because he believes there's a truth to this world that his God has laid out, but only a chosen few understand it. I'm also guessing he's shitty in bed.

Mary saw the problem in that logic. But still, she dated him. He must have been good for her or to her, somehow. I didn't have that answer for Tom, and I still don't have it for myself.

I step into the hall from the shower and Tyler's pacing. He stops and looks at me, a question all over him that he doesn't speak.

"What is it?"

I watch him look me over, the towel wrapped like my mother, but this isn't his first time at that rodeo. "I'm scared, Av. For real." His face bunches up and he looks like he's eight, not thirteen. "You think there's any chance he's coming for me?"

"Who?"

"The killer!" His voice rises up to the ceiling.

I had a feeling this was coming. Just like I know I'm in for it when I see Beth today. No responses from any texts last night. I even left a voice mail.

It's too much, all of it. My life is too much to begin with, and now this.

I sigh and reach out to Ty in the same way Dad and Tom reach out to me. I understand his fear, and part of me wonders if he's got a legitimate concern, but I say, "He's not coming for you."

"How do you know?"

"This has nothing to do with you. It's about Mary. It's about some psycho's hatred of me. Those things have nothing to do with you."

Tyler scowls. "That's bullshit and you know it." I try to protest but he keeps going. "You think I don't go to school and hear kids talking? That crap the other day about your junk, that's nothing. The shit I hear and don't tell you . . ." He pauses and, looks up. "Av, why does he hate so much?"

It's a punch in the gut seeing him like this, knowing how much he's suffering because of me. "I wish I knew, Ty." Then I lean closer. "Unless, maybe we're better off not knowing. Not like it's going to change anything."

"Don't lie to yourself, Av. Knowing why is half of Tom's job. Finding out the who is the other half."

He's right, and we have to leave it at that. I have to go to school and so does he, regardless of what we'll hear and we can't ever say.

❖

Officer Howard pulls to the side of the road to wait for me, as I slide into Beth's. It's surreal having him behind me this morning, but it was nice how he kept away the reporters who were camped down the street. Beth pops out of the door just as I put the car in park. I came here first instead of Charlie's because I figured I'd have to go in, have to put in some time apologizing. But then I see her parents at the window, peeking through the curtains. I wave. They let the curtains fall.

She gets in and buckles up. "What are you waiting for? Drive."

I don't argue, but when I pull away and the cruiser slides behind us, I see her face fall as if she just lost an argument.

"What is it?" I ask, not bothering with music this morning.

"Seeing him." She points at Officer Howard. "My parents were soo pissed last night. They don't want me to see you until the case is solved."

I'm not the slightest bit surprised. "Did you tell them what happened?"

"Of course I did, Av. They called the police station and all that. I think they talked to Tom. They're worried that if I'm with you, then I could be next."

"You sound like my brother," I say, and it comes out super snotty. "Sorry, I didn't mean it like that."

"Well, Tyler's smart if he's thinking that way. You, me, Charlie." She turns. "We are picking him up, right?" I nod and she continues. "Your family, shit anyone in this town could be next."

I ignore her hyperbole. "So that's why you didn't get back to me last night?"

"Because I was worried about my safety? Yeah, a little? And because you basically kicked me out yesterday."

"No, I didn't." I look away from her.

"Yeah, you did. When the conversation turned toward Mary, you wanted me out."

"All of you."

Beth throws up her hands. "Exactly! You can't do that, Av. I want to know what happened between you and Mary. It's important."

"Yeah, but it was different. I'm so different now."

Beth levels me with a cold, unaffected eye. "No, Avery. You have always been you, just like I've always been me. Sure, you're more mature. But you still had feelings then. You still loved her, right?"

The question chokes me up. I'm shocked at how raw I am, how easily this conversation turned to me playing defense, to me now being utterly defenseless.

"Yes, Beth. You knew that, though."

"Of course I did. And that's why I know you still do."

I pull the car over because I can't keep having this conversation and focus on the road. When I get to the shoulder, I put my hand out the window and give Officer Howard a thumbs-up. I don't need him pulling a gun just because I'm crying.

"What do you mean?" I ask Beth.

"I know you, Avery. I saw the way you used to look at her, the things you'd say about her. It was sweet. You still had feelings."

"Does that bother you?" I'm closer to being able to look at her, but I can't just yet.

"No. Most boys don't know how to love. You have more love to give than you know what to do with." She curls her hand into mine.

"What are you saying? Does that make me less of a boy?"

"That's not the issue, Avery. That's not *my* issue at all. You know that. All I was saying is that you have a wonderful heart. One that you hide because you have to. I understand that. It doesn't mean I can't see it. I see you, Avery. And I'm scared for you. For me, too."

I look at her now. Beth's face is dry and steady and she's so strong. I reach out and pull her to me and cry on her shoulder.

Once I'm good, I pull myself together and head to Charlie's. His dad's at the window again, shaking his head.

"What's he doing?" Beth asks.

"This is the shit he pulled the other day."

Then Charlie's dad turns, seems to yell something, and Charlie's flying out his front door. He pops into the back. "Go. Just go."

I do, but look back and see Charlie's dad still in the window, still pissed off.

"What's the deal?" I ask.

"Um, something like I need to stay away from you for eternity. Or at least until no one wants to kill you."

"I'm so glad your parents are on the same page," I say to the two of them. "But I'm pretty sure the flock said I'm going to hell, so that's pretty much getting killed over and over, for an eternity right?"

"Satan's an asshole," Charlie says.

Beth shakes her head.

"So, I've been thinking . . ." Charlie acts as if we're picking up where we left off, that all this fear of getting killed is nothing. "I'm betting your uncle didn't spill anything to you about the case, because, laws."

"Pretty much." I roll with it, because I'm already feeling emotionally drained.

"Right, so, then who do the two of you peg as the most likely killer? Because I definitely plan on doing nothing else in school until he's found. I mean, it's like the perfect excuse to do forensic work instead of math and English."

"Except, you can't really get to any evidence," I say.

"Screw you and your logic. I can still think, pick up the pieces that are available. Seriously, we know shit that no one else knows, so why not use that?"

Neither Beth nor I say anything. Not that it would stop Charlie if we did.

"So, Avery, if I go too far, tell me to shut up. I'm trying to block out the idea that this is Mary. I'm thinking of it as a case study. No name, no face. You know?"

"Gotcha." I wish I could do the same, but I know that until the day I die I will see that image in my dreams, and in those awful moments when my brain slips down the drain and asks for the dark.

"So based on what we've got, the guy has to be good in the woods, has to be comfortable with surgical instruments, and has to also be tech savvy."

"We're looking for a psychopath Paul Bunyon, who also happens to be a surgeon and an IT guy?" I look at Charlie in the rearview mirror.

"And don't forget religious, and transphobe," Beth says.

My brain puts up more check marks, but Charlie pipes up. "I wonder about that. The killer obviously knew Mary. So he'd know her family, and obviously knows the connection with her and Avery. Maybe that religious stuff was a ploy. A way to make everyone think Calder or Matthison."

Solid, solid thinking, but I'm stuck on the word *knew*. As in past tense.

"So, if not them, who?" Beth turns to Charlie.

"Well, there's that hunter. I dug online, and they released his name in an article. I searched for him, and guess where he goes to church?"

"Matthsion's."

"Bingo, Avery."

"But does he know me? That's the question."

"And one for you to find the answer to."

Beth shoots me a look but I pretend the road needs all my attention. "Right. I could do that. Who else, though? It can't be only him. Yesterday you were saying it was Calder."

"I was, and I still wouldn't rule out Calder, or even the reverend, but the more I think, the more they feel like long shots, so . . ."

"Why are they *long shots*?" Beth asks.

"I think, by this point, the cops would know if it were either of them. They've been interviewed, had their homes searched. If *anything* was found, the cops would have moved on that. We were all there yesterday, those guys are grasping at straws."

His answer makes me uncomfortable, because it's so smart. And, of course, he's not done.

"So there may be someone from your past that you haven't considered, Av. Someone who hates you. You've had a lot of weird encounters. Anyone stick out?"

That list could take me the entire day to write. There have been kids throughout the years who have beaten me up, threatened to beat me up, whose parents have done the same, all the religious nuts who think I've forgotten about God, and then the randos I've bumped into, who once they realized I wasn't a tomboy, managed to reach into the recesses of their brains, remembered the stories about the kid in town who believes he's a he, not a she, and then gave me all sorts of shit. But we don't have that kind of time.

And what Charlie and Beth have not brought up is the demand of that text. What I'm to do. My penance. This is someone who knows me and who knew Mary. And who managed to get so sick in the head, he murdered. Because everyone knows the way to change someone's soul is to kill it first.

So when I pass the reporters on the way into school and see the flock at the entrance, a prayer circle in full effect, I don't answer Charlie. I don't look at Beth or acknowledge Officer Howard. I walk straight to them. I haven't ruled out anyone, yet.

I listen as they pray and the words make me itchy, all the promises of things greater than the here and now that fly through the air. If that were so, then Mary wouldn't be dead.

"Hey!" I wait for them to notice me. They don't. "Hey!" I yell again. They stop and look up. Calder's with them. I stare into his eyes when I speak. "I need to talk about Mary. I need answers from someone. Now!"

Calder's face doesn't change. He looks as awful today as he has every day since Mary disappeared. Could it be him? Does he hate as much as he'd have to?

"Yeah, Avery?" Eva asks, suddenly at my side, her tone like she's talking to one of her ornery horses.

I open my mouth to tell her I want Calder. I really meant that I needed him to confess, but, instead I see her shirt. She has a button of her and Mary pinned to it. I look around the circle. They all do. Each with an individual remembrance. It's beautiful, and I hate them for having it.

"I need to know something, Eva. Could you answer one question for me?"

She sighs and grabs my hands. "I can. Ask from your heart."

I want to gag at how sickly sweet she is, and how desperate she seems to enfold me. "Who were Mary's enemies?"

I feel Beth and Charlie behind me. Probably Officer Howard, too. But Eva stays with me, focused, her face slightly upturned. "There's only one I can think of."

"Great. Who?"

Eva shakes her head and I think for a minute she won't answer. Then she smiles and says, "You, of course."

It's such a cheap answer, such a cop-out line in the face of my obvious need that I feel an urge to hurt her. I shove her back, away from me. "Fuck you!" I scream.

Officer Howard is suddenly on me, grabbing my arms, pulling me back. But I kick him and jump forward, back to the flock, who is now silent. Eva stands with her hands cupped before her, as if about to receive communion.

"You deserve to rot in hell. You hypocritical, pious, bitch!" I scream.

"Me? What have I done but told you the truth? Mary struggled because you were once her friend. But she came to understand that a wolf in sheep's clothing will always be dangerous." She stops, steps forward. "And I bet you still are."

It takes me a moment to consider what she means. Eva's not the sharpest knife, but she's not dumb. Put her on a farm and she's rustling everything into place. So I need to work through her animal analogies. "What are you implying?"

"I'm saying that someone like you would be willing to do anything so that people would believe your story that you're the poor lost sheep, instead of what you really are."

"And what's that, Eva? What am I?"

She crosses herself. "Only God can answer that. He sees with eyes that we don't possess. *You* wrote that on Mary's locker. Remember?"

Her words sting. I know it was an empty threat, another cheap shot. But at the same time, I know I'm not completely innocent. Without me, Mary still exists.

Eva steps back into the circle and the flock starts praying, again. The words wash over me. The hate I feel is diminished by my guilt. Or their faith.

This is why I hide. Up and down the hall is a sea of faces, looking, peering, prying. But at least they're not also talking shit, making fun of me, asking stupid questions. However, their silence may be worse.

With Officer Howard behind me, they look, but only so long. I imagine that he's staring them down, but that's unlikely. He has his orders, but I'm not sure if empathy is part of them.

Yet, as much as I hate everyone for ogling, I can't say I blame them. I probably would do the same in their shoes. This school has two reminders of Mary's death: the shrine of her locker, and the walking target that is me.

The whispers crawl over me: *He tried to kill Avery, too. Avery gets death threats every day. I even heard the flock praying for him.*

So when I slip into Luce's class, I try to be as discreet as possible. I slouch in my desk next to Charlie.

"This ain't hide-and-seek, Av."

"I know. I just want to pretend I'm not here. Like none of this is really happening."

"Story of your life, man."

This pisses me off, until I consider it.

Luce steps away from her door at the bell, seems to wonder what to do with Officer Howard standing there, but ultimately shuts it, leaving the sentry in the hall. She gives me a weak smile as she crosses to the front of the room.

She begins her presentation about fingerprint dusting as if there's absolutely no irony to the situation. I think about Charlie's comment, how this is all he's going to focus on. I might do the same. It could give me something to do aside from yell at the flock and wish I had an invisibility cloak.

Charlie and I get set around the lab table, looking for fingerprints on the objects Luce has given us: a can, a glass, a remote control, and a DVD. We have to find latent prints on two with the black light and two using a transfer card. We set to work and it's tedious, but the results are instantaneous.

If only it hadn't been raining, maybe Tom's men would have had similar results. I almost raise my hand to ask Luce about what we would do if it had rained or snowed, but I think that question would be so obvious that she might bounce me out of class.

I then have another, darker, and much more sinister thought: *What do you do with parts you've taken off a body?*

It isn't right, and it isn't healthy, but I can't control it.

Luce checks our results and is satisfied, and when she gives me another smile to downplay the obvious tension surrounding me, I speak up, "Can I ask you something?"

"Certainly, Avery? What is it?"

Charlie looks up as if he's only mildly interested, but I know his ears are recording whatever's next.

"All right, but please don't be offended."

Luce loses her smile.

"Let's say I wanted to preserve something, would I use formaldehyde?"

She crosses her arms. "Are we talking about a small animal, like the fetal pig, or frog?"

Charlie's eyes go wide.

"Similar. Yeah. Tissue and all that."

Luce thinks for a moment, and then time seems to stand still as I watch the realization spread across her face. "Avery!" she says, scolding, but mercifully low so others don't hear. "Are you asking what I think you're asking?"

"Maybe. Why?"

She sighs. "Because you shouldn't do that. You shouldn't look at this tragedy that way, like a case. Like you're just like everyone else around here, trying to decipher what they found."

Charlie, pointedly, looks away.

"It's difficult not to," I say, leaning close. "I'm sure you've heard all sorts of rumors at this point. Things about me, about Mary, about the case." I give Luce a chance to reply but she doesn't. "Thinking like this may be the only way for me to keep my head on straight. Because if I think about it, really let it in, the pain is too much, Mrs. Luce."

"And what about the answer to your question isn't going to hurt?"

"Because if it could help, then the pain's worth it."

She nods at this, looks around the classroom, and then back at me. "Don't say anything more. Just listen. I don't want to be part of your theory. Okay?"

I nod.

"There's an officer outside for a reason. We all know that. So don't pull me into this." She pauses, looks at me, and must accept what she sees, because she goes on. "Yes, you would use formaldehyde."

"Is it tough to get?" I ask.

Luce inhales so quickly her nostrils collapse. "I told you not to say any more."

"Okay. Okay. Thank you."

She turns away and when she does Charlie looks at me. "Nicely done." Then he holds up his phone. "If your uncle takes this again, we might have some explaining to do."

On the screen is a website with a checkout page for a bottle of formaldehyde. One click and Charlie would be able to possess what I believe the killer already does. Because I know enough to grasp that the odor of a decomposing human body is pretty wretched, I understand that something would need to mask it, especially if the pieces were meant for future use.

We start packing up with more time left to class than is necessary and Charlie uses the opportunity to spew his thoughts: "I bet you could search for local purchases or deliveries of formaldehyde." "I bet he bought containers, too." "Unless he already had some." "All right, I may need to back date the formaldehyde purchases . . ." And on he goes. I nod and say "Mm hmm," when appropriate, but that's about it.

The killer has reached me through my phone twice now. No amount of formaldehyde or purchase orders can make a difference in that. I wish I knew someone with tech skills. Someone who could decipher how these messages are untraceable.

As if reading my thoughts, Officer Howard steps into the room. The class freezes at the sight of him, but he ignores them and waves me over. "Out in the hall," he says.

"What? Why? I'm cleaning up. The bell hasn't rung yet."

He swats my words away. "Your uncle is out there. Needs to see you. Now."

My broken heart falls into my stomach and my hands are so weak as I go to the door. Tom being here could be good news, but so far that hasn't been the case.

He's standing at the end of the hall, looking out at the track and football field. When the door clicks shut, he looks at me. "We need to talk," he says.

I want to say *no shit*, but I keep the snark to myself. "Officer Howard said that."

"You okay after yesterday?"

"Yeah, I'm awesome. How about you? Did your captain appreciate what I could provide?"

Tom swallows and stands straight. "Now's not the time for that. Have you received any more texts? Has he reached out to you in any way?"

"Do you really think I would keep that to myself at this point? Beth and Charlie and Tyler are all afraid they might be next. Tom, I'm coming to you with evidence as soon as I have it. Whether it's any good or not."

He frowns at this. "We're working on that. The phone must be a TracFone. Or multiple TracFones. It's more complicated than you think."

I didn't mean the comment to ruffle his feathers, but I'm not that upset about seeing him this way, either. "I believe you, really. But why did you call me out of class? Officer Howard could have easily given you every detail of my morning."

Tom looks down the hall to my class. "He's a good officer. You're protected. That's all that matters."

"And everybody else? Like my friends, my brother, my family? What about them?"

"For right now, there's no reason to think anyone else is at risk. But there is an officer at the middle school. Tyler's safe. If we need to do more, for Charlie or Beth, we will."

"So just me. And the Matthisons are being tortured by this freak's desire to keep the hunt going, to keep leaving pieces of Mary on their doorstep. Or is it some sick game the reverend's playing? And Calder, what about him? He's just good to go?"

Tom shifts his weight. "Avery, if we had reason . . ."

"What about the hunter?" I cut him off.

Tom looks confused.

"You know, the one that found Mary. He's a member of Matthison's church, you know. Could be a connection there. If he hates me and hates something the reverend said."

Tom puts up his hands. "What are you saying? Listen to yourself. He had no reason to come to us. But he did. And he's a mess over it. He is quite honestly haunted by what he found."

"Is he? Or is it just an act?"

Tom levels his eyes on me. "If it's an act it's a pretty amazing one, because he's in the hospital receiving treatment, and yet somehow those body parts that were taken keep getting dropped off."

I see this hunter, some grizzly looking dude with a beard like Charlie wishes he could grow, sitting in a hospital bed, chillin'. I still don't know if I buy his innocence. He could have an accomplice, someone who . . . I stop short, the thought twisting back to what Tom said.

"You said the body *parts* are being left. Did it happen again?"

"Avery, stop. That's sensitive information."

"Bullshit. Half this town already knows. Sure, they may not have the exact details, but they know enough. The integrity of your investigation sucks, Tom."

"And what would you know about that? What, you take some forensics class and then you think you can do my job? Is that how it works?"

"So far, yeah."

Tom recoils, the anger coursing through him. I'm happy to see it, thrilled that someone else is as upset as I am. Because losing Mary like this is a fucking tragedy, having the killer still on the loose and playing games is a goddamn nightmare, and the dawn never seems to be coming.

Then Tom stares at me, through me, and refocuses. "Mary's ears were hanging off the front porch when Reverend Matthison went out to get the paper this morning."

I take a step back and run into the lockers.

"Yeah. Exactly, Avery. That's how this case feels, like I'm getting shoved around. So I'm sorry if I shove back, but I think we're all on the same page at this point. You know things you shouldn't, but I have no control over that. The killer wants you dead. He wants to torture the Matthisons until that's a reality or until you repent." Tom steps closer to me. "And repent for what, Avery? You haven't said. What did you do?"

Eva's comment comes back to me and I hate how right she is. "Nothing weird, Tom, don't worry. I didn't do anything *freaky* with my fucked-up self. You know what I did do? You want to know what sick and twisted thing Avery Chase did?"

Tom says nothing, but everything about him screams that he wants the answer. "Mary, who was murdered and mutilated, I loved her, Tom. And she loved me back. It's that simple. And whoever this monster is, who has these pieces of her, he knows that. So you'd better think again about some poor hunter who had a *feeling*. Someone truly sick and twisted and smart and capable had to have done this. Not many people in this town fit that description, least of all me. So get looking where you may actually find something."

"I am, Avery." His tone is grave. "He's left the second piece. You know what that means."

"Yeah. Mary's mouth isn't far behind." That image turns my stomach.

Tom nods and his head looks so heavy. "True. But it also means that your time is coming."

"What the hell do you mean by that?"

"Exactly as he said. You either repent or you're next."

I turn away, can't bear to look at him as he speaks. Can't bear to believe that he just went *there*. "You put a police officer on my ass twenty-four/seven and you're telling me that you think I'm still in danger?"

"No. Maybe."

"Which is it?" My voice echoes down the hallway.

"Avery, try to focus, stay with me. All I'm saying is that if you do what he asks, then you can guarantee your safety. That will buy us time to keep looking."

And find nothing, I think but don't say. He should know better. He should know me. Clearly he doesn't.

"Don't ever ask me to do that, Tom. Don't even think it."

"Avery, be reasonable. I've spoken with your parents about this. They agree that if the choice comes down . . ."

"It's not their choice! This," I say, pointing to myself, "is not a fucking choice!"

"Avery, Avery, I never said it was."

"But you did, and you are right now. Giving in to this psychopath, dressing like a girl or some shit. That would be like death. And honestly, this guy killed someone, and you want me to play along with his head fuck? That says more about you than it does about me."

"I'm trying to protect this town, your friends, your family. Didn't you just say that you were worried about them? Well, if you're so worried, then yeah, I am asking you to do what has to be done. Just because you're playing along doesn't mean you agree. It just means that you're willing to sacrifice. Is that so bad?"

We could stand here all day and argue back and forth about what this request is, but it would get us nowhere. Tom is too far down this rabbit hole to see any other perspective but his own tunnel vision. Find the killer, solve the case, the hell with how it's done. I understand. Part of me feels that way about transitioning. I am who I am, and if it's testosterone and binders now, and top surgery down the road, then so be it, regardless of the cost. What I don't know is how that makes me right and him wrong, but it sure feels that way.

The clock in the hall ticks and the bell is about to ring. My phone chimes and I wonder if it's Charlie, checking on me. No doubt this argument has stopped all productive education in this hallway.

I read the text: *You should listen to your uncle. Better the devil you know . . .*

That is one hell-of-a-messed-up thing for Charlie to say, and I go to fire back a response. Then I see who it's from. Not Charlie.

"Tom?"

"Yeah, Avery?"

"Tom, you need to read this."

It could be the wave my voice rides or the fact that I'm holding my phone, but Tom doesn't ask any questions, just pulls my cell out of my hand. "Is this? Is this either of the other numbers?"

I shake my head and see in his eyes what I imagine is in my own: pure fear.

"He's listening to us," Tom says.

"Tom, he's probably in this hallway."

He pulls out his walkie-talkie. Just as he makes the connection, the bell rings and a surge of kids enters the hall. Whatever Tom was planning to do is washed away by their movement, the killer or his spy hiding among them.

Tom grips the walkie-talkie again and screams into it. "Lockdown! Put the school into lockdown!"

Kids nearby hear him and look panicked. I consider my options and then see Charlie coming my way. "Back to Luce's," I say.

"We're going into lockdown? What happened?" Charlie watches Tom, who is still barking orders.

"You heard that fight?" I ask.

"Uh, yeah. Hard not to."

"You weren't the only one."

"What are you talking about?"

"Go to Luce's. I'll explain."

He scratches his beard and then heads back from where he came. Tom's off the walkie-talkie, face contorted. "Why haven't they called it?"

"Probably won't happen until everyone is in their next class." I look down the hall and see what he sees, kids taking their sweet-ass time, hanging at lockers, or oblivious to it all, faces glued to their phones. "We're sitting ducks, Tom. I'm heading back to Luce's. If you need me, find me."

At that, Howard is at my side. Tom says, "There's no way I'm losing sight of you. Go. We'll catch up later. But this could take a while."

I head back to class and Officer Howard comes inside with me.

Luce is gawking at the commotion of my uncle. "Avery, what's going on?"

"Lockdown, Tom said."

"A drill?" she asks, but in a way that's rhetorical.

"Prepare for some quiet time." I leave my teacher and find Charlie.

"What's the deal?"

I hand him my phone. He reads the text. "That happened while I was fighting with Tom."

Charlie's shoulders twitch. "Damn, I just got a chill from that. So, he's here? He's one of us? Calder?"

"Maybe," I say, and before I can elaborate, our principal's voice comes over the loudspeaker.

"The school is in lockdown. I repeat, the school is in lockdown. This is not a drill."

The air takes on a frenzied quality, as teachers pull kids into classrooms and then lock their doors. Lights are switched off, and everyone goes silent.

Charlie and I slide into a back corner so we can whisper. We're not supposed to speak, not supposed to be on our phones. Potentially, our last breaths should silently be taken in the stuffiness of a second-floor forensics lab.

"What do you mean by *maybe*?" Charlie says as soon as we're settled.

"I think it's possible it's Calder, but I also think it's possible that it's someone on the outside and he's got an accomplice, some spy here, who could be Calder."

"Why?"

I shouldn't share, it's confidential and all, but too fucking bad. "He left Mary's ears at her parents this morning."

Charlie stares at me, and I'm guessing he's seeing those pictures again, how awful a human looks without ears. How butchered Mary was. "The fuck."

"Exactly."

"So, kind of hard to be in two places at once?"

"Sort of. I don't know if they have an exact time when they were left. That's something you could do overnight and then come to school the next morning."

Charlie's chin is on his chest. "What? What are you saying?"

"I'm just trying to think like the killer. Wasn't that going to be your job?"

Charlie closes his mouth, pulls his knees closer. Luce looks us over and kids quiet. Their whispers are all about this being connected to the case. They're not stupid. And if so, then how could the killer just walk among us? It's just not possible. Or is it?

Our principal comes back on the loudspeaker. "Ladies and gentleman. I need you to listen and then I need your utmost cooperation with the directions I am about to give." He pauses. "You are to return to the class you had previous to this period. Teachers, take attendance and then e-mail the office with your roster. We are still on lockdown. There will be no instruction, no talking, and no use of cell phones. You will face punishment if you violate our code of conduct. Return to your classes now."

I check my phone and every social media site is already blowing up about the fact that we're in lockdown. The reporters outside are losing their minds. Some are even suggesting an arrest is imminent.

Luce comes over. She looks at Charlie and then at me, as if hedging whether it's okay to speak to me in front of him. She makes up her mind. "Avery, is this at all connected to the conversation you had with your uncle?"

"Why? Were we that loud?"

Luce says, "No," but Charlie nods.

"Totally," he says.

Shit. I can't imagine how much was heard. And by how many. Whatever Tom's trying to do with this reorganization isn't going to work. There are too many students, too many ears listening. This town is too keyed up for any bit of information. And there we were, arguing about Mary's murder and suspects and evidence. Based on what I'm seeing online, plenty was heard and shared. Tom may have just shot himself in the foot.

A wave of noise comes from the hall. Like the beginning of a fight. Officer Howard moves to the door and locks it, unconcerned about the kids trying to get out or in. He's here for one person and I haven't moved. But the noise grows louder and now seems to be coming from outside. We all move to the windows.

Kids cover the sidewalk, like an ant colony streaming from its nest. They run away from the school, some to cars, some to waiting parents, who are bug-eyed and dumbstruck. It's barely 10 a.m., and the shit has hit the fan.

The reporters madly set up cameras and begin live coverage. I'm sure daytime programming is now being interrupted by what's going down, just as much as I'm sure Tom is watching all this play out, with more rage and impotency than anyone else.

❖

School's unofficially out, but I can't go anywhere. Officer Howard won't let me. Tom's orders. Fortunately, Charlie's with me.

Beth texts: *Where are you?*

Luce's. I can't leave.

Shit, you're my ride. I'm coming to you.

I don't reply, there's no point in stopping her, and since I'm going to be here until Tom says so, the more the merrier.

"Can they even give detention to that many kids?" Charlie asks.

"Please, this town would go batshit if they tried," I say.

Luce plops down in her chair with an audible sigh. I want to ask her what she's thinking, but I decide it's best to leave her be. Then there's a knock on the door, and Officer Howard crosses the room.

"It's my girlfriend," I say, but he ignores me and turns to the door. He opens it, but stops her. "Arms to the side."

"What?" Beth says as she steps into the room.

"Like I said." Howard isn't messing around, and Beth doesn't either. We watch as she becomes a scarecrow and is then patted down. She squeals when he gets a little too close while in between her thighs, but it's all over within a few seconds. "Thank you," he says.

Beth rolls her eyes and joins us at the window. "This is nuts. I was in English and then all of a sudden someone said, 'Just go for it,' and the entire class bolted. I stepped into the hall with Mrs. Dela-croix and it was a river." She looks at me. "What happened?"

"Why are you asking me?"

"Really? Even down there we could hear you and Tom."

"Like specifics, or just us?"

"No specifics. It was like when your parents fight and you're in your room. Little pops." She tilts her head. "Oh, right, your parents don't fight, do they?"

They do. Plenty. Especially about everything related to my transitioning. Well, at least they used to. I think once I got to high school and committed to the testosterone and binder and short hair, they understood. It took Mom a while longer to be Team Avery, but I get it, she was losing her little girl. She already had her little boy with Tyler. And I think all the hopes and dreams she had for us: shopping, talking about boys, proms, and weddings—all that shit that girls have their heads filled with—she wanted that. Regardless of how I feel, I took that away from her. Not my fault, but still.

"What day is it?" I ask, completely ignoring Beth.

"Thursday," Charlie says.

"No, date. Sorry."

"The twelfth," Beth answers. "What's up?"

I feel like an idiot for saying anything, but where my mind went just reminded me of where I need to be tonight, since it's the second Thursday of the month.

"PFLAG tonight." I look out the window. "Right about now, I could use talking to kids who get it."

"What does that mean?" Beth asks, and stands a little to the side.

"Shit," I say, then smack myself. "I forgot to show you." I hand her my phone.

She reads. "What? When did this happen?"

"That's why Tom is here. He came to talk to me and this came through while you were all eavesdropping on our fight."

"Avery, you're not actually thinking about doing what this asshole wants, are you?"

"No. Not a chance. That would be like . . ."

"Being someone you're not," Charlie finishes. "See, we get you." He points between Beth and himself.

I want to tell them that, yes, they do, but only to a degree. They're the best cisgender people I know, but it's still not the same. It never will be. I'm okay with that, because I'm on the inside looking out. But it won't always be that way.

Tom busts through the door and keeps me from having to go into that conversation right now. "Avery," he says, "go home. Officer Howard can escort you now."

Officer Howard shoots Tom a look.

"There isn't anyone to interview. They're all gone, in case you didn't notice."

Officer Howard nods and stays mute.

"Tomorrow. I have names. We'll find out what we can."

It sounds like he's saying this more for himself than for Howard's benefit, but if I were Tom, I think I'd be talking to myself nonstop. He leaves and we follow Officer Howard into the hall.

It's as quiet as it is over the summer. I've been in for so many meetings to discuss my accommodations that this is weirdly nostalgic, and at the same time very surreal. This town, all our lives, everything has become altered since Mary went missing. And now? It's going to be pure pandemonium.

We step into the daylight and reporters crowd in as close as possible.

"Avery? Avery? Can you tell us what your uncle said to you? What instigated this walkout?"

I stop in my tracks and stare in the direction of whomever just spoke. "What?"

"Can you confirm that Mary Matthison's killer is now coming for you?"

Beth tugs on my arm, but I don't budge.

"How do you know that?"

"So you are confirming this. Is it because you are transgender? Does that have anything to do with the murder?"

My brain rattles for words, because some part of me knows I am going to be on TV, and what I say will get composed into a sound bite, so it had better be good. Beth tugs again, and I see Howard doubling back to get me.

And then another thought flickers: *I bet the killer will see this.* What better way to send a message.

"I'm Avery Chase and I loved Mary Matthison. Whoever did this is an animal and deserves the justice coming for him."

I walk away, and sure as shit, a moment later my phone chimes. Beth and Charlie look at me. They must have heard it, too. I pull my phone from my pocket.

Justice is coming for us both.

Dad hugs me as soon as I walk in. "Avery, thank God you're all right. I saw the news, and then what you said. Tom called and confirmed everything." I think he means to say more, but he either stops himself or can't find the words. He pulls me tight to him again. I hate that in this moment I think about my boobs squishing up against him, and how I wish that weren't the case. I hug him back, though. He needs this more than I do. Because, yeah, I'm scared and angry, but I also remember how haunted Reverend Matthison looked. If he didn't have anything to do with Mary's murder, then Dad's on the verge of feeling the same as he did. I never want that for him.

We separate and I see an officer out the back door. "How long has he been here?"

"About a half hour." Dad looks out the front, where Officer Howard is stationed, again. "I don't think I ever want you leaving the house." He looks me over, as if seeing me in some entirely new light. "What happened today? Why did everyone run out? It looked like Columbine."

I reach for my phone to show him the answer, but stop. "When's Mom going to be home?"

"Any minute now."

"Tyler?"

"They're releasing them for a half day, so it should be a half hour or so."

I take a deep breath, I think the first I've been able to all day. "Well, let's wait for them before I answer that."

Dad looks in my eyes, and I see his pain. Parents really do get the short end sometimes. "I love you, Avery. And I know that there are two cops outside willing to shoot down this monster, but please know that I am willing to take a bullet for you."

"Dad." It's all I can manage before I lose it, and slump to the floor, much like I did when Tom came with the news about Mary.

Less than an hour later, the entire family is home. Tyler and Mom hugged me just like Dad, and Mom cried, and Tyler might have. It's all gone a little blurry. We sit at the table and I answer the question Dad asked when I came in.

I take out my phone and they scroll through the texts. They've seen the pics, except for Ty, and so I quickly move past them. "And so that one you're looking at," I say, "that's the one I got when Tom and I finished arguing at school."

"What does it mean, Avery?" Mom asks. "What were you and Tom arguing about?"

I can't believe I have to say this, but it's the truth of my life, so I spill. "He thinks that I should do what the killer wants, play along, dress like a girl or whatever he means by *repent*."

Both my parents' hands go to their mouths, which I take as a good sign.

Tyler shakes his head. "I heard that, too."

"How?" I ask. We're not even in the same building.

"I don't know, it just exploded all of a sudden. I think maybe someone got a text and then it was everywhere. We then saw video of the school emptying, and we thought to run, too. But there were guards at every door."

"What is going on?" Mom says, sounding very much like Mrs. Luce.

"So, you and Tom argued about this, and then you got that text?" Dad asks.

I nod and see the conclusion pressing firmer into him.

"He really is watching you, then?" Mom asks. "That last text, that came after you said what you said on TV?"

"You were on TV, Av?" Tyler's excited for a moment.

"Yeah. Somehow those reporters know I'm a target and then they asked if it's because I'm transgender. What the fuck?"

Ty shoots me a look like I give him when he swears.

"I meant, what the hell."

Mom throws her head back. "No, what the *fuck* is right." She returns her head to level and glares at my father. "What is your brother doing? How in the world can everyone know everything about this case?"

In her question I wonder if they really do. "Did you hear what happened this morning? You know, *why* Tom stopped in to see me?"

My parents stare blankly, their answer obvious.

"He left Mary's ears at the Matthisons', just like he left her eyes, right?" Tyler says.

Now my parents look between my brother and me, horrified. "Yeah, he did. How do you know that?"

"Like Mom was saying, like today at school, it's everywhere, it's all anyone's talking about."

"Then how hasn't he been caught?" Dad slams his fist on the table and we all jump. He sees this and apologizes. "I'm just upset and scared. I mean, if this twisted animal can have this much influence and seem to be everywhere at once, how can I possibly feel like you're protected, Avery?" Dad swipes a hand over his face. "We should go somewhere. Get out of town. Take a trip. Something. We need to get away from here."

There's silence as we all contemplate this. It sounds like a smart move, the intelligent thing to do, but I feel as if I have to be here in order for the pieces to fall in place. And without all of them, the killer could stay in hiding. So does that mean that I'd also have to hide forever, too?

Tom comes through the front door without even knocking or ringing the bell. He sees us around the kitchen table and doesn't look for a chair.

"I'm guessing Avery told you what happened?" Tom says.

"Yeah." Dad's turned to face him, his face growing red with his anger.

"You have every right to be pissed, Gordon."

"Thanks for letting me have my feelings, Tom." Dad's snark is fantastic.

Tom hangs his head and Mom speaks up. "We're just upset. Avery shared all of what has gone on, all the texts. Is he really coming after him?"

Tom looks back up, but before he answers I snatch my phone back. "You didn't see this one yet." I walk to him and hand over my phone. "Right after I said what I did on camera, I got this."

Tom reads and then hands me back my phone. "Jesus fucking Christ!" Tom kicks the bottom of the wall. "He *is* everywhere!"

Dad stands. "Tom, it's okay. We didn't mean to upset you."

"You haven't, Gord. You're my family, and this is my job, and somehow Avery has come into the crosshairs. And I don't know what to do." His voice drops during his last sentence, sounds a lot like mine, like it's so fragile it will break.

"But you do, Tom. You have to have suspects at this point. Bring them in. Keep Avery safe. You'll catch a break."

He puts up a hand. "Oh, we have suspects, but we have absolutely no evidence tying any of them to Mary or to the scene." He looks at us, who are all gaping at him. "I shouldn't be telling you this. I should leave."

"No!" Dad grabs Tom's arm. "I don't care if we all go to jail for talking about this, tell us what you don't have." Tom struggles but Dad holds on. "Tom, Avery's life is on the line."

Tom struggles one last time and frees himself. He growls and then stares at the floor. "You repeat

any of this, and I might as well shoot myself. Got it?"
He doesn't give us time to answer. "There's nothing.
Nothing on Mary's body. Nothing at the crime scene."

"So was she moved there?" I ask.

Tom looks up.

"I told you forensics was a good class."

"Yes, we think she was moved. And before you
ask, yes, we've investigated the Matthisons', Calder
Riley's, and the home of the hunter who found her.
Nothing."

"But you have pieces. Did you look for formaldehyde?"

All heads turn toward me.

"He's got to be using it, to preserve the . . . parts.
Or they'd reek."

Everyone's still looking. No one's talking.

"What? It's not like I'm okay with this," I say.
"Charlie and I were talking about it. We figured you
should look for purchases or deliveries made for
jars and formaldehyde. Even if you start with those
three suspects."

Tom swipes a hand across his face. "We already
did that. Good call, though. The parts have been
covered in it."

I'm sickened and amazed by my intuition, or
intelligence. "And I'm guessing no one's had any
delivered. And I'm assuming you've checked the
school's lab as well."

Tom shakes his head. "Good work, Avery. I
should enlist you. No deliveries and all is accounted

for at the school." He chuckles to himself, the laugh of someone at the end of his rope.

"We know what enlisting Avery's help means," Dad says. "That's not going to happen."

Tom looks confused, but then seems to remember. "You've read the texts. You understand how this is going to play out. Once Mary's lips turn up, what choice are you really making by not playing along?"

"You can't be serious?" Mom says.

"I am. Think about it. We have every possible resource on this case, but we've come up empty. We have a body, which is an enormous piece of evidence, but so far all it's done is given us even greater opportunity to get more evidence, because pieces of it keep showing up. And still, nothing."

"Install a camera on the Matthisons' house," Tyler says.

"Already have." Tom smiles at my brother. "Maybe you should both work for us."

"Uh, no. Not if by working for you means I have to wear a pretty dress," I say.

Tom looks at me. "If it comes down to you wearing a dress or you wearing a coffin, which would you choose?"

Mom gasps and Dad says, "Tom!" but they wait on my answer.

"How about you do your job so I won't have to make that choice." I walk past him and head up to my room.

I've texted both Beth and Charlie to see how they are, but neither has gotten back. I bet Charlie's dad took his phone again. No doubt today's news will have him under house arrest. But I highly doubt we'll have school tomorrow or anytime in the foreseeable future. We'll catch up.

Our school and the kids fleeing are all the news has been tonight. Along with shots of me, of Tom and of the captain. This town is upside down, and I understand if that means Beth needs a moment to breathe. Her parents are cool, but everybody has their limits.

And I've kind of reached mine with the people around me. I meant what I said earlier, that I need to get out, go to PFLAG.

When I head downstairs I see that Mom's trying to ignore the television by folding clothes. Dad's helping her, and there are maybe two towels completed between them.

"So, I'm going to the meeting tonight, just wanted to let you know."

"What? No. You're not going anywhere," Mom says.

Dad just blinks and blinks like he's a fish.

"I need to. Really, I do. We don't have school tomorrow, right?"

"No. Got the robocall a little while ago."

"So I'll be housebound all day and for who knows how long. Give me a couple hours. It's not like I won't be protected."

Dad comes around. "He makes a good point. He's probably the safest person in town."

Mom fluffs the T-shirt on her lap and then gives a small head shake. "I don't like it, but fine. Keep your phone on you at all times. I'm going to text as much as I want."

"That's fine. I should be back by eight thirty."

"Be safe," they both yell as I head down the hall to the front door.

Officer Howard turns when I open it. "I'm going to a meeting. Want to come?"

He straightens. "Where to?"

"PFLAG. You heard of it?" No way he has.

"*Where* is it?"

"Oh, right." I give him the address, which, fortunately is in another town. It's not like there are PFLAGs everywhere. I'm lucky to have one even this close.

Officer Howard radios where he's headed to somebody and then talks to the officer out back, who then comes around front. We exchange looks, but he says nothing. I hop in my car and my shadow follows.

PFLAG is good, but it is not an ideal organization. I think I was in sixth grade when Mom found a chapter just outside town. She seemed excited for a support group, so I pretended to be excited with her. All it took was an online search to stir my trepidation, but I went anyway, and my concerns were supported within the first five minutes of the first meeting.

The full name of the organization is Parents, Friends and Families of Lesbians and Gays. I am none of those things. Yet Mom felt solace in speaking with families that live on the fringe, like we do, yet strive for a weird normalcy that will never be achieved. It's kind of sad, really, that pressure.

Over the years, though, the group has opened up to other trans kids, like me, and has provided a bit of a bridge with us and the gay and lesbian community. We are all at different places on the spectrum of gender and sexuality, and PFLAG is the one place that seems to get that.

I park at the church and the irony is astonishing. Just fifteen miles away, Matthison oversees a congregation that sees all gays and transgender and queer people as abominations. Really, anyone who doesn't fit the binary of cisgender and heterosexual. Whoever runs this church may still think we're going to burn in hell as well, but at least they have the decency to allow us a place in which to cry, to share stories, and to eat cookies before we do.

Officer Howard follows me inside, but stays in the foyer when I enter the meeting space. Everyone notices me at once. "Avery!" is a collective shout. And then they crowd. I feel bad for the newcomers, because it's not typically like this. They're all "Are you okay?" "Is there anything we can do?"

I wish there was something they could do, but the support alone feels good. I've never made friends with anyone in the group, because it's easier to be stealth when you're alone. Or maybe that's something I say to myself to make me feel better about being scared to open up to others.

Ms. Prentiss steps in the middle, sweeping her silver dreads to the side. "Come here," she says and holds me close. "I'm praying for you, baby."

"Thanks," I say and feel choked up. She must sense this because she tells the rest to back up, give me space, and take a seat.

"Don't worry, I won't let it be all about you and what has happened. We're here for you. We're not paparazzi."

I take a seat and we all give Ms. P our attention.

"Thank you, everyone. We're going to begin as always with the teens here, and adults in the next room." A few parents say things to their children and then cross into the next room where they have someone else leading a discussion for parents only. Then Ms. P sits in the circle of chairs and continues. "For those of you who are new, we start with introductions. I am Ms. Prentiss and have been a loud and proud lesbian for over thirty years." She turns to the girl next to her. "Please, Melanie."

This girl, with a pixie cut and loose jeans shrugs. "I'm Melanie and I'm a lesbian. I came out of the closet two years ago. Yeah, I'm uh, sixteen."

The next girl goes and then the next few boys, and I don't recognize any faces that are trans. It's all right, because the company here is good, but still.

When it's my turn I say, "My name's Avery, and I'm transitioning from female to male. As far as I know, I'm hetero." The group chuckles at this. "I started transitioning around middle school, and am currently on testosterone therapy."

"So no periods?" one of the girls I don't know, asks.

Ms. P shoots her a dirty look. She has rules about this stuff. We don't ask about the parts, the function of things, unless the person brings it up and *wants* to share. But the girl seems genuine, so I answer.

"Nope. Only had to experience that a couple of times."

"That's the shit right there." The girl smiles wide, and I smile back. It's the absolute truth. Nothing made me feel more *female* than that.

After introductions, Ms. P opens the floor for discussion. The conversation, as usual, revolves mostly around issues at school, issues at home, and how to best protect oneself. Ms. Prentiss offers advice here and there, but mostly allows the group to run itself.

A kid named Jeff says, "It's not that people don't accept me, it's just that they have these weird ideas about how I'm supposed to be. You know, like, what I'm supposed to do. And when I find myself doing those things—caring about fashion, gawking over some hot celebrity, whatever—I get angry, because I don't know if I'm doing this because that's who I am, or if I'm living up to their stereotypes." He looks around the group for support and there are a lot of nods and "Mm hmms."

I'm one of them. I understand *exactly* what he means. I bet a whole lot of other people would, too, if they'd let themselves.

"Jeff brings up an excellent point," Ms. Prentiss says. "This question of conformity versus identity is so prevalent. However, I want you to think about how much your hetero friends or family deal with the same issues. Don't they also have to come to terms with who they are versus who the group wants them to be? Especially if they have a tight group of friends or play a sport or are in other extracurricular activities. We have jocks and preps and goths as much as we have gay and lesbian and queer."

It's as if Ms. P has gone back on her word and has made this about my life. About Mary. It's strange to think of her, here, in this place, in this context. But she was just like any one of us. That day in the water signified more than just a feeling for her. She acted on that, and by doing so, acted against her church and all the things she'd been bred to believe. She acted from her heart, and then her father crushed her for it.

I wonder how she kept those feelings suppressed for all these years. Was Calder a beard of sorts, or did she just settle? Did she still have feelings for me? Because I sure as hell still had feelings for her. Still do.

I find myself leaning forward to speak. "Except, we also have gay and straight and queer among the jocks and preps and goths." My voice is strong and deep. I simply love how it sounds. "And we have them in youth groups and in the pews of places like this. How are they, I mean, how are *we* ever supposed to know where we begin and the other influences end, especially when they force us to hate ourselves?"

The group considers, heads nodding, comments made to one another. Ms. Prentiss turns to me, putting me squarely in her focus. "That is an eloquent point, Avery. Could you elaborate on from where it came?"

I straighten in my chair. "For those of you who don't know me, or saw me on TV today, I'm from West Center. We've just been in the news because there's a murder investigation underway." My voice catches. "The girl murdered, Mary. Well . . ." I can't. I thought I could but I just can't bring myself to say it.

"Go on, Avery, say what you need to!" someone yells.

"We got you. Let it out!" another says.

I know they do. I just have to trust. I swallow. "Mary was my first love. Way back in third grade. And all the way through. We even kissed once. My first. And she was a reverend's daughter, and there's so much wrapped up in that fact, and my uncle's the lead cop on the investigation." I pause, look up. "It's horrifying. And with such anger, I'm worried, about myself, about anyone on the outside. There's a difference between tolerance and acceptance."

There's quiet contemplation when I'm finished and I'm glad I made it through to my point. Prentiss looks like she is as well. Then Melanie speaks. "I have a cousin there, and she says it's just nuts. She also says that reverend is real anti-gay."

"He is," I say, and have to restrain myself from saying more.

"Then maybe this is Karma biting him in the ass," one of the boys says.

"Excuse me?" Prentiss asks him.

"I'm just saying. You preach hate and bad things come back on you, don't be shocked."

The room recoils at this. "So you're saying his daughter deserved to die?" the kid next to him asks, and I grip my knees as if I'm trying to pull out the bone.

"I'm just saying that maybe this reverend, who-ever, bears some of the blame because of what he preaches. Maybe someone who hates what *he* stands for turned it on him and hurt him in the worst way possible."

I feel as if I've been stabbed in the stomach by this kid's point. Why haven't I thought of this? Who in our town would want to see Matthison pay?

Conversation continues about religion and school and all of who we are. It's a difficult con-versation and one I find myself tuning in and out of. *Everyone has enemies.* And yet I never thought of the reverend.

This killer had to have hated Matthison or he wouldn't be torturing him like he is. And as I think of that, think of having your child murdered and then having pieces of her left for you to discover, I erase Matthison from the list. Unless it's one hell of a deception, or some act of contrition for the guilt he feels, there's simply no way.

I feel as if what Tom said today, repeatedly, that they have nothing, is so disturbingly wrong. The evidence is there. He's just not seeing it.

Looking around this group, I wonder what they would do in my shoes, give in to the killer or stay true to themselves? But maybe giving in isn't what it first seemed. Maybe it's not what the killer perceives as true, but what I do. And if I can provide Tom some slack, give him an opportunity to dig deeper, then maybe he can go far enough to find an end to this nightmare.

I stare at the search bar, mug of coffee at my elbow, tiny cigar burning in my lips. I don't know what to type.

The house is dead quiet, how it should be at 4 a.m. When I woke, or really just decided to give in to my insomnia, I opened my windows and looked down at the officer out front. "You mind if I smoke?" I asked.

He shook his head. "Just don't ash on me."

I then went and made coffee, came back to my room, and lit a strong chocolate-flavored cigar. If my parents wake up and yell at me, too bad.

But even with the caffeine and the tobacco I don't know where to start. Wide awake when I should be dreaming, living this walking nightmare.

"Burners," I say aloud, and then type how to use them. It takes a bit of tweaking the search, but I find an article that perks me up. I sit up straight and read about burner phones, but then I find that instead of buying disposable phones, there are a dozen apps that do the same thing, and that some are untraceable.

"Tom wasn't kidding," I say. This could explain why all those texts from the killer are from different numbers. I'd put money on the fact that he's using the same phone and then burning the number each time. How in the hell is Tom going to catch that? And they've already looked at the homes of the suspects and he knows about the formaldehyde. Am I wrong to think that's there's something he's not seeing?

I cup my head in my hands and feel the cigar burning down toward my finger. Part of me would like to stay like this and let it burn, let it singe me, let it start a fire and put me in the hospital. Kind of like the trip Dad teased earlier. But this way I could be drugged and completely out of it while the search goes on. They could even do top surgery while I'm there, so when I come out, if the killer's still on the loose I can laugh at the fact he wants me to dress like a girl.

I slide my free hand up and under my binder, feel the swell of breast there. B-cup probably. The testosterone should keep them from growing. It better. I reach down my pants and slide my hand into my underwear. The throb that went dormant when Mary went missing has returned. As my hand slides over my swollen parts, I realize I need release. I need a moment away from my life, from this darkened path it has become.

I close my eyes and I think of Mary. I have a thousand images of her in my mind, a plethora of ways she looked beautiful to me. Her body, her smile, the light touch of her hand. I consider all this as I start jacking off, and then I fall back to my stand by, her that day. That day that changed everything.

She ducks underwater, and when she emerges her suit is wet and clinging to itself, exposing more than when she was dry. But it's her eyes that draw me in. They are magnetic. What she sees, she wants to devour. And my face sits squarely, reflected back.

I stroke harder now. I drop the cigar and am frenzied by my imagination.

Because now Mary is kissing me, like she did that day, her soft lips hungrily sucking, and her teeth nibbling on my ears and neck. But now she slips her hands inside my shorts, and she doesn't find what was there. She finds what should be. And she strokes as I stroke now, and the water churns around us. I delicately slide my fingers into her, and the moan she lets out makes my legs quiver.

We stand in the sunlight, two people helping each other feel what it's like to live, to love, to give and to receive pleasure. The water warms around us, and we both reach climax and shudder.

I open my eyes, and my desk sits before me, cluttered with my ideas, my burning cigar and a computer screen filled with the here and the now. My breathing is shallow and my heart is racing like I've been sprinting. I sit back, grab the cigar and take a long draw. My exhale creates a fat cloud that is whisked quickly out the open window, just like my memories.

I shower at 6:00 and make my way downstairs, acting as if I only had trouble sleeping, instead of the truth: it was an impossibility. Dad gets me a mug of coffee, looking as bleary-eyed as I feel.

"Rough night?"

"Yeah. I couldn't stop thinking."

He sips from his mug and then says, "We can always take you to Dr. Hathaway. I'm sure he'd prescribe something."

Some people have a pediatrician. I have a team of docs, and Dad knows I like my psychiatrist best. Even exhausted, he's good like that.

"If it continues, I'll think about it."

Dad sips some more coffee and checks on the eggs he's making. Mom walks in and is surprised to see me. "No school and you're up at this hour?" She doesn't wait for an answer, though, but hugs me. It may be more of what I need than Dad's suggestion. I let her hold me for longer than usual, and she's a little misty-eyed when we pull away. She rubs my back, and I sit at the counter.

"What are you going to do today?" Mom asks, grabbing her own coffee.

"Don't know. I don't have any homework or anything. Probably binge on Netflix or something."

"Well, if you want to get together with Beth or Charlie, go ahead. They can come here, or you can go there. Of all days your father has a meeting."

I'm surprised by this, considering I have a killer stalking me. "Really?"

"Yes, really," Dad says.

"Your father and I know it will only make it worse for you if we keep you locked up. *You've* done nothing wrong." She drinks from her mug. "Plus, as you've said, you are protected at all times."

"Thanks, Mom."

Dad slides a plate of eggs and toast in front of me. "Eat. You're too skinny."

I laugh and dig in and wonder whose house I should go to first.

My parents eat and chat and try to make the morning seem as typical as possible, and then Dad says, "Are we going to the meeting tonight?"

Mom frowns and I see her look sideways at me.

"What meeting?" I ask.

Mom's full on shaking her head now. "There's a town hall meeting. Tom let us know last night while you were out. We're going to discuss . . ." She trails off, genuinely seeming at a loss for words.

"I think we're going to discuss everything. Like when to begin school again, the case, the safety of everyone in town," Dad says.

"Does Tom want us there?" I can already feel the weight of the conversation. How the undercurrent will be: *if we just get rid of the freak and his family . . .* What then? I don't think they know. Because they'd still have a killer among them.

"He didn't say," Dad says. "What do you think?"

I sigh into my empty plate. "They're going to have the conversation about me whether I'm there or not. I might as well throw in my two cents."

"But that's it, Avery." Mom has regained her composure. "You can't slip and divulge anything about the case."

"No shit, Mom." I push back from the table. "But

what if I did? What would I tell them that they don't already know?"

I stomp out of the room, not caring if it wakes up Tyler, if it jostles the cop at the door. I wish my stomping could wake the dead, or pulverize the rest of my body.

After my parents leave, I text Beth. Nothing. I text Charlie. Nothing. I'm going to have to go over. It's possible that Charlie's dad took his phone to work with him. But Beth? Her lack of response is starting to scare me.

I head to Tyler's room. He's still sleeping, sprawled all over the place. I shake him awake. He's so out of it his eyes flutter but clamp shut again. "Ty! I'm going out. Mom's at work and Dad has a meeting. You're fine. Someone will be on the house all day. Okay?"

His eyes open. "Where are you going?"

"Charlie's and Beth's probably." I rub his head and turn to leave, but he grabs my arm.

"No."

"Ty, what are you doing?"

He uses my arm to pull himself upright. His eyes bug. "I had a dream, Av." His voice is deep and doesn't belong to the little boy I know.

"It was about Mary," he continues. "She was calling for help. All alone in the woods. Running, I think she was barefoot and kept looking over her shoulder." He stops and shakes. "It felt so real."

I sit next to him. "It's all the details of the case. Your brain's just putting them into a story."

"Maybe," he says, "or maybe it's a sign."

"Like what?"

"Like maybe Tom missed something. You know," he says and scooches closer. "Like maybe it was her ghost."

He's so serious it's difficult not to laugh. Why would Mary's ghost come to him? As I think about it, I realize I'd be crazy jealous if that were the case. How sad is that?

"Okay, well, maybe. I mean, the woods are deep and who knows how much could be out there? Tell Tom tonight. There's a town meeting."

Ty nods and rubs his eyes. "I will." He then stands and pulls on the jeans he left crumpled on his floor. "Give me a sec, all right?"

"For what?"

"I'm going with you. There's no way in hell I'm staying here all day, cop or not."

I want to argue, but don't have the energy.

A half hour later I pull into Beth's driveway. Officer Howard tucks his cruiser onto the shoulder. "Stay here," I say to Ty. "This is private."

"Sure thing." He pulls out his phone and I walk to her front door.

The curtains flutter and I worry that her parents are home. But the cars aren't here, and a second later Beth opens the door. "Hey," she says and wraps her arms around my neck.

We kiss and then I ask her, "So what's the deal? Your parents take your phone or something?"

"No." She crosses her arms over her chest. I note this and her lack of explanation.

"So you chose not to reply?"

"Yeah. I think it's a good move, considering."

"Considering what? You're not a target."

Beth leans against one of the porch posts. "My parents don't see it that way, and to be honest, I agree with them."

I'm floored. Just yesterday she needed to be with me when the shit was hitting the fan, and now? "So what does that mean?"

"It means until the case is solved, until you don't have a killer coming after you, until you don't need a police escort, we can't see each other."

I lean back against a post, because if I don't I'm going to fall over. "Where is this coming from? Is this your parents?"

Beth reaches out to hold my hands, but I tuck them up under my armpits.

"Avery, listen, I still love you, but I can't do this right now. It's too much."

"What is? The case or me?"

She stills and looks me square in the face. It's unnerving how similar her eyes are to Mary's. "Don't do that. You know the answer."

"Do I?" It's automatic, because I believe I do know, but something about this moment demands that I ask.

"Who else do you have, Avery? Charlie's your only friend, and I think we can safely say he's mildly fucked up. And you have me. How do you ask that question?"

"What, do I owe the two of you medals for being my friend and girlfriend? Are you somehow special because you're *willing* to be with someone who's transgender?"

Beth's face blossoms red. I brace for her anger. "How dare you say that? No, I don't want a medal, but you should recognize that being with you isn't the same as being with someone else. Yes, it is more difficult."

"You knew that when you hit on me." I point at her, accusingly, and immediately wish I hadn't.

"So it's my *fault*? It's on me that this is a tough relationship? Because I was just telling you the *case* is what's making it difficult. You're going down a different road with all this."

Arguments swirl around my head. Things I should say, things I know I should never say. But I'm exhausted and fragile and my normal restraints have long ago fallen away. "You say it's the case, which pisses me off. It's *Mary* we're talking about. But really, you know it's more than that. Because if you can't support me now, when I need you the most, then fuck you. If this is too difficult, then walk away, Beth." I pause, try to control my voice. "I thought you were different. If I was wrong, fine, I made a mistake, but at least I own that. You want this to be something it's not."

"What's that?" Beth's voice is a flame.

"Easy. You want it to be like it is for all the straight, *normal* kids." In spite of her anger, I lean in. "It will never be that way. After Mary's murder is solved, I will still be different. That's not my fault."

"Again, it's mine?" She throws up her hands.

"No, but it's the price of admission that I thought you were willing to pay. I thought you were better than the rest."

"No! You thought I was like Mary."

Everything stops. The world is simply frozen in place. My vision is reduced to a white-hot tunnel, and at the end is Beth. I want to hit her. I want to lash out in some way to hurt her as much as that statement hurts me. But I do the one thing I know will be the worst of all. I let my silence speak for me. I let her know that she's right.

❖

Tyler didn't say a word when I got in the car. He just looked me over and then buckled his seat belt. I was glad he was quiet and I was glad he was there, because he kept me from spinning doughnuts on Beth's lawn. He kept me from ramming into a telephone pole. He kept me from going to Charlie's. Because if I heard another lame ass excuse like Beth just offered, from him, I would have gotten back into my car, and in spite of Officer Howard being on my tail, would have driven into a ravine. Mary's gone. Beth's gone. Charlie's in the wind. If it's just me and a killer on my back . . . If it's just me having to make that choice . . . If it's just me . . .

I pull into the police station and when I get out of my car, Officer Howard looks thoroughly confused.

"What's going on, Avery?" he asks.

"Need to see Tom," I say.

"You could have let me know, I would have radioed for you."

I'm surprised by his friendliness, but also concerned that I'm so out of sorts I'm misreading him just doing his job. "Thanks." I head inside the precinct.

The desk officer opens his mouth, but then changes direction. "You two here to see your uncle?"

"Yeah. Is he around?"

"I think so." The cop picks up a phone. "Chase here? Tell him his nephews are out front."

That word: *nephews*. That's all I want this town to see. Why is it so difficult?

Tom comes through a side door. "What's up?" He looks as tired as ever and almost as old as my father.

"Av's kind of a mess right now, Tom. Could you help us out?"

I'm surprised to hear Tyler speak so bluntly, but am also happy he does.

"Yeah, let's go inside. Av, you need a coffee?"

"About ten," I say.

We follow Tom into the break room and sit at the cheap tables. He pours me coffee and gets a soda for

Ty. Then he sits down. "What is it? Something happen?"

I go to answer but then think about what happened yesterday, the interviews Tom was going to run, the research I did this morning. "Why aren't you talking to the kids from school?"

He frowns. "Have to get their parents to agree to it first. Have to get them on the phone before that. Seems nobody in this town wants to take my call."

"Shit," Ty says and drinks his soda.

"Probably wouldn't have helped anyway," I say.

Tom leans back in his chair. "Oh yeah, why's that?"

"Burners. Or a burner app. Dude's untraceable."

Tom lets his chair fall back down. "How do you know that?"

"You ever heard of Google?"

He looks away and Tyler leans to me like he's going to say something but doesn't.

"Sorry, Tom, I'm not here to piss on your work. I just thought of something and wanted to run it by you. I also think Beth and I just broke up, so if I sound like an asshole, my apologies."

He nods. "Av, I'm sorry to hear that. I think you and Beth work well together. Maybe after the pressure of the case is over, you could try again."

I feel tears working their way out, so I squeeze my eyes tight. Tom's a good man. In spite of everything, he's still giving me dating advice. I clear my throat before I speak. "Well, it's something I was thinking about, how whoever did this must have hated Mary. But I can't think of a single enemy she had. And then I realized the killer must hate the Matthisons, too. I mean, what he's doing, leaving the parts, that's just sick and twisted."

"It is, Av, but what's your point?"

"Who are his enemies? The reverend. Who hates him enough to do this?"

Tom stares at me, his mind running behind his eyes.

"He preaches a lot of hate. He ever piss off someone so bad that they'd go after him? You know he also used to hit Mary. Anybody get wind of that and go to him? Maybe he took it out on her? Maybe then he had to cover his tracks."

I realize what I've said goes against everything I've been thinking, but after this morning, maybe I'm right to second-guess it all.

"Av, are you saying what I think you're saying?" Ty asks.

I ignore him and look at my uncle, who hasn't moved a muscle. "The evidence is there. You're just not seeing it. Look past the obvious. Go deeper. This isn't some simple case. I know you know that. Mary was an angel, and yet someone hurt her. Because of me. But why? To get even, or to get revenge?"

Tom grabs his own coffee, slams it like water and stands. He's out the door before I think to ask about the meeting. I hope whatever I said spurred something in him. Something to allow him to see the impossible.

We get home and my eyes are watery from all the yawning I've been doing.

"You need to take a nap," Ty says. I couldn't agree more. Then my phone chimes and the surge of adrenaline jolts me awake.

I check the text. It's from Charlie. I almost drop my phone I'm so happy. *Hey, you going to the meeting tonight?*

Yeah. Where you been?

Dad made me go to work with him. I stole my phone back while he's getting lunch.

There's still hope. Charlie's still got my back. *Sorry. Hope he gets over his anger.*

He's scared. But FML, his job is sooo boring. See you tonight.

Beth's words echo back. Yeah, maybe Charlie is a bit messed up. He was weird before his mom died, and after, he didn't get any less weird. But why should he have to? When this is all over, I'm going to do what Tom said and see if her issue is really about all that's happened, or if it's something else. Because she really does deserve credit for her willingness to see me. I couldn't say it when I was on her porch, I was so angry. But she's different than Mary, and better in so many ways. I've been putting Mary up on this pedestal, and that's not fair, especially to Beth. She took the first step into this relationship, and I know that took guts. She's been the highlight of the past year. And I fucked up. I have to apologize, to tell her she's right.

We walk inside and I head upstairs. Ty keeps going toward the living room, so I stop. "Hey, thanks for your help."

He stops, looks up. "What'd I do?"

"You were there for me. You helped with Tom. You didn't pry about Beth."

He leans against the wall. "Av, if I didn't do that shit we'd have a problem. You're you, and if people give you shit for that, that's on them." He pauses, and I'm amazed at how mature he sounds. "Maybe I'm just used to things, but isn't that kind of the point? Things are only weird if you don't understand them. Really, if you don't try."

I'm about to fall into a million pieces over his insight. "Damn, Ty. When did you grow up?"

He smiles, but it's a sad one. "When did you forget that you're Avery Fucking Chase? No way can you let some psycho scare you, whether that's Calder or the reverend or someone else."

My heart fills with his words, and I know not to speak because I would cry. I fist bump him through the air, turn and head to my room.

Sleep comes in fits and starts, like I'm a fussy infant who can't get settled. Maybe it's trying to sleep during the middle of the day, but I wake and stare at my ceiling and fight not to pick up my phone and text Beth or research something forensics related. Or read every post about Mary, every stupid theory, including the ones that say she's still alive.

I roll to my side and pull open the bottom drawer of my nightstand. I have a few pictures in here, ones from my childhood. They help remind me. I see myself with long hair and the silhouette of curves beneath my oversized T-shirt. Mary's at my side, and we're both happy to just be there in that moment in front of Mom's camera.

Another, and I'm older, the smile fading along with my curves. A new glint in my eye that has nothing to do with happiness, but rather the beginning of understanding. Mary has something similar. But in her Sunday dress and pigtails, you'd never know how dark.

The last is of only her, taken secretly with my phone, one day last year when she was too gorgeous to get out of my mind. I hold the picture within an inch of my face and stare. This is how I want to remember her, not the ways in which I can see her now: dismembered and discarded.

Tears burn and my throat aches. But the pain that drives through me is not over losing her this way, it's losing her before, it's regret. I should have been more careful, more watchful. It's not as if she changed. She was forced into a mold that she was *supposed* to already embody, by a father who used any means necessary—Bible or belt. On one level I know how she felt, how regardless of the effort to work within the confines, you never feel like yourself, who you really are.

I knew about the punishment. I knew and I did nothing. I knew, more than anyone else, and I let her get washed away with Calder and look pretty for her father's cause and say words from a Bible she only half felt. How could I?

I stick the photograph to my chest, at my heart. I press it there, as exhaustion takes over, and I feel myself falling asleep. "Please forgive me, Mary."

We park a street away from Charlie's house and I text him to let him know we're here.

"Why are we doing this, again?" Dad asks, but I think it's just to fill the silence. He knows Charlie can't be seen with me.

A minute later Charlie opens the door and hops in. "Hey, Chase family. Thanks for the ride." He closes his door and Dad drives.

"Anytime, Charlie. How's your dad?"

"Same as always, pissed off."

The town hall is within the stretch of buildings downtown with restaurants, bars, shops, and a real estate office. Our police escort provides us with a space close to the hall, in spite of the sea of cars covering the square.

We hear the noise as soon as we step out of the car, and it only grows as we get closer. The doors are wide open and people line the steps to listen. Someone at a microphone says, "You've repeated the fact that there is no present danger to any of *us*, but you haven't answered why you think this, or how you know. We've watched the news, so we know what you're saying isn't true."

A rapid round of applause fires while Charlie and I make our way through the crowd. We stand against an uncomfortable outcropping of the wall, and my parents and Tyler file in behind us, with Officer Howard flanking our every move.

Heads turn and some stare. But, fortunately, with the discussion going on up front, we don't have to suffer their glares for long.

"Thank you for understanding that you are, indeed, safe, but please remember that this is an ongoing investigation, and so I cannot divulge any elements of this case that could jeopardize its outcome. And we all know that the media has a way of twisting the story." Tom is no politician. His words are sensible and articulate, but he delivers them with all the grace of someone being forced to apologize. Someone in the crowd yells.

"So you're saying that your nie . . . I mean, nephew, isn't at risk? Or are you saying he is the only one?"

Those heads turn back now, and I have no choice but to look away.

The room bubbles with conversation and I hear my name a few dozen times, along with the hatred: *Fucking freak, Queer, Dyke*, as well as offers to *turn me back into a girl, fuck me so hard, I'll turn straight*. This is when Beth would squeeze my hand, but Beth's not here, and I find Charlie staring out over the crowd. I follow his gaze. Calder is sitting with the flock, which is surrounding the Matthisons.

"What are you thinking?" I ask him.

"Nothing. Just watching. You can learn so much from body language, right?"

"Yeah, what are they saying?"

"Nothing. Yet."

"Can you at least tell us who your suspects are?" someone yells. I search for the speaker but can't find him.

"Please, let's have all questions at the microphone. We want you to be heard," Tom says, and the crowd laughs at him. The man who spoke was obviously heard, but more than that, there's no respect. This *we* is him and the captain, who's standing, arms crossed, as if on guard. His eyes are invisible under his hat.

Tom shifts his attention to him, speaks at an angle and the crowd stirs. Tom pops up and returns to the crowd. "Let's have some words from Captain James." Tom extends his arms as if this is some beauty pageant and he's the emcee.

He's impressive in this venue. Very well built and as steady as a support beam. Completely dissimilar to my uncle who is now leaning on a nearby podium as if it's a life raft.

"Officer Chase has given you all the information he can. There is very little else I can offer, except to say that I have worked on similar cases in my career, and Officer Chase has done everything by the book. Obviously we will continue to investigate the case and update you as necessary."

"So why are we here? What's the point?" Another shouted question.

"I will reiterate what Officer Chase has said. If you feel you have seen something, or if you know something, call. If you aren't sure what you remember, but it's nagging at you, call. If there's even a shred of doubt that something you've heard isn't just a rumor and may, in fact, be connected, call." Captain James pauses. "However, if you just want to check up on us or ask how we're doing, put your phone down. You will find out along with everyone else when we catch our criminal. We all have the same goal, and I promise you, we will reach it."

There's a lot of head nodding at what he's just said. He sounded just like a high school football coach, which made sense since this town operates on that wavelength. But he just tossed up a whole lot of white noise to distract people from the fact that he's basically told them to sit tight and shut it. I respect what he's doing and what Tom's going through, but I am a target. That's been established. Maybe the town hasn't been clued into this. Maybe they should be.

The microphone is ten feet away and it squawks when I grab it. Someone makes a dick joke, which I ignore.

"I'm sorry if you've already addressed this. I came late. What have you said about the killer?"

A wave of whispers crashes around the room, and not just the standard insults. This town isn't ignorant, just biased. But here I am before them, seeming to be on the same page. Let's hope Tyler's right and I really do know what I'm doing.

The captain looks at Tom, and the anger is apparent. But he's on the spot and this is our town. Someone needs to answer the question. James clears his throat. "Could you clarify the question, Avery?"

"Can *he* clarify a lot of things?" someone else yells. I wait to see how the crowd reacts, but there's less laughter than I expected, so I forge ahead, clarifying only what matters.

"Should we be looking at an outsider, or is the killer one of us?"

The room erupts in conversation. I look over at Charlie, expecting an enormous grin, but he seems as shocked as the rest of the room. I turn away and catch a glimpse of Calder. Eva is holding his hand and speaking directly in his ear.

Captain James coughs, I think in an attempt to control his anger, or to silence the crowd. At least the latter occurs. "Based on the evidence, it would seem that someone with substantial knowledge of the Matthison family as well as the terrain near their home and the surrounding woods fits the profile best." He stares at me.

I shouldn't continue. I should listen to the seething pleas to step away from the mic, coming from my parents. I should step back and ask Charlie what's got him freaked. But I don't. Something in me won't allow that.

"Thank you, Officer James, but you didn't really answer the question. Any hunter from around here, who also attends the reverend's church could fit that description. I'm wondering how close in proximity. Could it be someone in this room?"

The crowd erupts again, as they should. That was a terrible question to ask, but I needed it to prime them for my next.

Captain James is speaking to Tom, clearly pissed off. Tom's shaking his head. At least he's being honest. No one here can answer my question. At least not until he's seen the plan through.

"Sorry, one last question, and then I'll get out of the way." Shockingly, the crowd quiets as my voice booms over them. "What's your plan after the last piece of Mary turns up?"

There's a gasp from the entire room. It might as well be the room itself. They're not yelling or arguing with each other, because I've just given credibility to the rumors. The very reason the kids ran from the school is out in the open and before them now. There's nowhere to run if they want the truth.

The captain and Tom are locked in a tight conversation. Dad yells, "Avery, stop!" But I take advantage of my leverage, this audience.

"Maybe they don't need to answer because we already have our suspects." I look around the room. They're hooked on my words. "I know *they've* ruled out the man who found the body, so we can check him off the list. But, in spite of us not being detectives, we all know the statistic about whoever was the last to see the victim usually knows what happened."

This creates a stir, because there's no rumor about who was last with Mary. Everyone knows that it was her father and then Calder. And we all know that she was upset.

"So, Calder, Reverend Matthison, care to shed any light on what happened?"

The reverend hasn't turned his head to look at me, to dignify that I actually exist, so I stare at Calder. Eva is beet red next to him, looking like someone stole her horse. Calder's eyes are dead. There is no scarlet in his cheeks. When he speaks, his voice sounds feeble, out of use, but ferocious. "I have no idea who did this, *Avery*. Yes, we had a fight, and I wish, every day, that we hadn't, that the last words I had with her were, I love you. So how dare you accuse me?"

I swallow, and in spite of how much I feel for his pain, say what I came to. "Because it's about time someone did." I don't wait for his reaction so that we can have a round of verbal tennis. I don't wait for the audience to get up in arms and derail this train. I continue. "The same is true for Reverend Matthison."

I watch the reverend. He sits, stoically, still not acknowledging me. "He used to hit Mary. Did you know that?" The room is eerily quiet now. It's like

I'm onstage delivering a monologue. It's frightening as hell, because I am so grossly exposed. But this is for Mary, and for her I'm willing to pay the price. "When she talked back about the church and about its hatred, he used a belt. That's not religion, that's hypocrisy."

Matthison stands slowly, with the practiced air of someone who believes that the rest of us are beneath him. Someone who honestly thinks the voice inside his head is God speaking.

"And the son said unto him, Father, I have sinned against heaven, and in thy sight, and am no more worthy to be called thy son." Matthison glares, as I've seen him do behind his pulpit and in his own home. Eyes so wild they're borderline hysterical.

"Hate me all you want, Reverend. Try and tear me down with all the Bible passages you can think of. It won't change the fact that you did what you did to Mary. Nor the fact that I loved her, and that she loved me. And now she's dead. Not because of me. Because of you."

His eyes smolder. "How dare you speak about her. I should cut out your tongue."

"And you probably could."

The crowd is a live wire now, pulsing with this idea. I brace for a punch or a slap, someone from the flock to tackle me to the floor. But it doesn't come. Instead, they rise.

"Righteous *art* thou, O LORD, when I plead with thee: yet let me talk with thee of *thy* judgments:

Wherefore doth the way of the wicked prosper? *wherefore* are all they that deal very treacherously?" The flock holds hands as they speak. They look at me the entire time, and I know in my soul that people have died with these as the last words they've heard.

Then, as with one voice, they pray: "Moreover if thy brother shall trespass against thee, go and tell him his fault between thee and him alone: if he shall hear thee, thou hast gained thy brother. But if he will not hear *thee*, *then* take with thee one or two more, that in the mouth of two or three witnesses every word may be established."

I look around the room, and the focus has shifted from me to them. The crowd's eyes glisten with approval, and when I look to see if Tom or the captain are going to do anything about any of this, all I see are two men who look as defeated as I feel. Dad pulls me away from the microphone and out the door while the meeting turned prayer circle continues. "What the hell are you doing?" Dad yells. We're down the steps and around the corner away from the onlookers on the stairs. I see Officer Howard fall in behind us.

"Just saying what no one else will." My breathing's erratic and I feel like I might pass out.

Dad throws his hands up. "Are you kidding me with this? You believe it was Matthison or Calder who killed Mary? And you call them out like that in public? With your uncle at the helm of this case?"

He pauses, looks me over. "What the hell is wrong with you, Avery?"

Dad never speaks this way. He's always been calm and collected, even when facing down the powers that be, trying to help them understand. He never lost his cool. "You don't believe me?" I ask.

Dad turns away. "Avery, please, that's an unfair question. I have no reason to believe you, nor anyone else for that matter. We simply don't know enough. So doing what you did is only going to get you hurt."

"You mean more hurt, Dad. I'm already a mess."

Dad grips my shoulder. "I'm talking about getting killed. That is a very real threat, like you said. Like Tom's said. You have to be careful. You can't reveal facts about the case. Who knows what unintended consequences that could cause?"

"They're all a bunch of hypocritical assholes. They hate me already."

Dad's face tightens. "Don't say that."

"What?"

"Avery, this is a crazy world where people die every day because of their beliefs. Yet we live somewhere that allows us to believe whatever we want, be whoever we want to be. You're the hypocrite if you don't see your hatred as equal to theirs."

There's truth here, but it's buried under a heap of bullshit I can't believe I'm hearing. "You have got to be kidding me? I *can't* be *me* because of people like them. *They* are responsible for all the narrow-mindedness, all the hatred that has been heaped on me ever since I understood who I am."

Dad steps closer and brings his voice down. "You're right, Avery. The harshest critics have been from the reverend's church. But that can't be surprising to you. Their beliefs won't allow for understanding. But somehow, Mary did. So there's hope."

The conclusion he just drew is killing me, so I'm glad he grips my shoulder. The support as much as his words is needed.

"Very soon you will leave this town. You will go away to college. Probably somewhere far away, somewhere you can reinvent yourself. And that's good. But you'll find the same closed-minded people there as you do here. You are going to have to be careful how you deal with them. Confrontation isn't always the solution."

I turn to him. "So what are you saying? Don't fight for myself?"

He pulls me close. "I'm saying be smarter about *how* you fight. I love you and I want you to become whoever you are, so don't let the here and now stop that. We've already lost Mary." He chokes up on this, and I hug him so hard the pain feels necessary.

When my father and I separate from our embrace, I look around to get my bearings. Cars line the streets, but we're mostly alone. The town hall is a beehive of activity. I can feel it humming with whatever has transpired since we left. They'll be streaming down the steps soon, maybe looking for me, maybe not. I wouldn't be surprised if the diner gets filled with people who want drinks and time to talk about the meeting. Others will use that gazebo, and many, I'm sure, will just stand out here under the moonlight.

I wish I felt the same. But I don't really want to say another word. I want my bed, and I want to stay in it forever.

My family joins us, along with Charlie, who keeps looking over his shoulder as if someone is following him. "Let's get out of here," Mom says, and no one argues.

With help from Officer Howard, we're out of the town square and on the road in no time.

It's quiet in the car, especially compared to the hall. And as much as I want to absorb the silence, to enjoy the calm, I need to see what's what with Charlie. I whisper, "So what'd you think?"

He looks toward my parents and shakes his head.

"Come on, they can't hear us."

He shakes his head again, and I ask Dad to put on the radio. He does, to one of their stations, but the background noise is all that matters.

"So?" I say nudging Charlie.

"That was a bad idea, Av."

"Why? It got the message out there, got them thinking." I check on my parents to see if they're eavesdropping, but they seem locked into their own conversation.

"Yeah, they're thinking, and probably a lot of bad shit about you."

"But they already do. How has what I did changed them?"

Charlie looks away. "Nothing unites people like a common enemy."

"Who said that?" I ask.

"No clue. But who gives a shit, it's a solid point. Sure the flock had problems with you, but you just called out Matthison before the entire town. He's their leader, and regardless of how fucked up they are and how awful he was to Mary, he's still got a wall of protection because of them. What do you have?"

"You," I say, hoping for a laugh, but Charlie looks like his stomach's turned sour.

We pull into his driveway and I hop out with him. "Hey, did they decide about school?"

"Yeah. We're back after the weekend. Granted nothing else happens." He looks at me when he says this, like I'm going to cause something new to happen. I don't know what in the hell he's thinking.

"You want me to swing by tomorrow then? Or do you think your dad is taking you to work on a Saturday?" I mean it as a joke, but Charlie doesn't take it that way.

"No clue. But, either way, I think we should just lay low for now, for a while."

"What the hell is that supposed to mean? You sound like Beth." And it dawns on me that I haven't told him. "Speaking of," I say.

"Don't bother, I already know," he cuts me off. Charlie must see the giant question covering me. "She texted. Wanted to make sure I watched out for you." He pauses. "She still cares for you. She's just scared."

"So she said. What about you?" My body tenses when I ask, as if it's preparing itself for the hit that's coming.

"You know, Av, I've been good up until tonight. That shit you just pulled wasn't cool. And I don't think it will make anything better. I know you're upset, and trust me, I know I've been leading the charge to find answers, but tonight wasn't the place. Seeing the flock like that, it reminded me of Mary's funeral." He pauses. "It reminded me a lot of after everything with Mom. It's not the same, but back then people expected Dad and me to get back to normal, to move on. It was impossible. Still is." He looks back at our car and then steps closer to me. "I don't know, seeing them and feeling the weight of their sadness was too much. And then you just smacked them in the face. How'd you expect them to react?"

I can't believe what I'm hearing. "I thought we were on the same page."

"We were, but not like that. Besides, the shitty way you acted, revealing that evidence, it isn't going to help at all. In fact, I think it will only make things worse. Like I said, now you have the entire flock riled up."

"So sorry to ruffle their feathers, but I think Mary's death is worth it. I also think that me being a target makes it worth it."

Charlie straightens. "I think you being a target should knock some sense into you. After seeing them tonight like that, it has for me. We need to keep our noses out of this, Av."

"Why? Why now?"

"It's you, Av. Maybe he was just toying with you before, but now maybe he's going to bring it. Clearly Mary's death has something to do with you and I think with the reverend, too. But you needed to lay low on this shit."

"But I didn't because I'm sick of being the transgender kid, who is supposed to hide out and not stick it in anyone's face. This is too big to lay low on."

Charlie's forehead pulls down. "Is that what you think?"

"Yeah, because it's the truth."

Charlie's face smooths out and he looks up. "No, it isn't like that. You hide because you feel protected that way. You're afraid of people more than they're afraid of you. And then the one time you really expose yourself, you attack."

I've been punched a few times in my life, but none of those hits have had as much impact as

Charlie's words. Is this how he sees me? "But you just said . . ."

"It's a two-way street, Av. Sorry, but yeah, the burden's on you. That's shitty, but what can I say."

"I think you've said enough."

Charlie turns and makes his way toward his house.

I watch him go and then ask, "So are you still Team Avery, or are you Team Beth now?"

"It doesn't have to be like that, Av. But I'm Team Charlie." He walks into his house, and I feel like I'm in one of those postapocalyptic movies. There's no one else in the world but me. I'm utterly alone, but I know I'm not. There's danger lurking. It is everything now.

❖

My parents ask if everything is okay when I hop back in the car.

"Yeah, fine. We were just talking about what to do tomorrow." They either go along with the lie or didn't actually hear us, because they both nod along like all is good.

Then Mom turns in her seat, to me, while Dad pulls out of the driveway. "Where was Beth tonight?"

"Sick," I say, and can't look her in the face.

Mom says something about sending her soup. I tune her out because if I don't, I'll lose my shit. All I can think about is Beth and Charlie, texting like they're the ones dating, deciding to cut me out of the picture because they're afraid I'm bringing this danger onto myself. Or are they afraid I'm bringing it too close to them? How fucking stupid can they be? Stupid enough to think I need them. They'll see. I'm going to help figure out this case. Help Tom get this monster. We'll see how they feel about me then.

We pull into the driveway, and the lead cop goes inside while we sit and wait. He clears the house and then radios Howard, who lets us out of the car. The first cop is in position in the back by the time we step out and onto the driveway.

Tyler says, "Av, hey, I still got your back."

It feels like he's been reading my thoughts, but I realize it's not that, it's just him being aware and attentive. Which is exactly how I should be. Having my head up my ass helps no one.

We reach the front steps and Dad turns to say something to Tyler and me, but waves it off and goes inside. Mom follows him, and Officer Howard takes up his position. I feel the weight of the day settle over me, and in spite of my nap, cannot wait for my bed. I hope to sleep like the dead.

I step and notice something off about the mums Mom has in pots out front. There's a dead mouse or something lying on top of one of the plants. Which makes no sense, whatsoever. I lean in for a closer look.

The dead mouse is actually a white-and-blue tinged blob that has an unnatural sheen, like an enormous slug that's started to dry out. I look closer, but don't have to. The smell hits me before I get a handle on what I'm staring at, and I know where it's from.

"Is that? Are those?" Tyler asks, his voice at my ear.

They are. To cut off the lips so that they retain their shape, the incision must trace under the nose, out to the cheeks and then down to the chin. The appearance is as if someone has cut away the bottom of a Halloween mask.

Mary's lips, identifiable by the tiny freckle at the left of her bottom lip, are slightly open, as if about to speak. And if they could, I'd listen, even though I know how horrifying the story would be.

Officer Howard's face goes from placid work mode to unreadable cop face in the moment he realizes what Tyler and I are losing our shit over. "Get in the house, now!"

He all but throws us in before snatching the walkie-talkie from his shoulder and screaming into it. Howard wrenches the door shut and continues screaming.

Mom and Dad appear, shocked white. "What is it? What happened?" Dad asks.

I'm speechless and look to Ty. But he's worse off than me, almost as bloodless as what we just found. I swallow hard and find my voice.

"Her lips. Mary's lips are on the front porch."

My parents shake their heads so hard it's like they're having an attack of some sort. Mom screams, "No!" but it's halfhearted. They know this has been the pattern all along. Only now the location has moved.

The coincidence of this is striking. The fact that this is on the heels of what just transpired at the town hall speaks volumes. Just an hour ago I was out in the open, I was speaking on Mary's behalf, about what lies on the flowers outside. And now, where I've always felt safe, the monster has come and laid claim by taunting me. He could get to me whenever he wants.

And now that the last piece of Mary has surfaced, it's time for me to repent. *See no evil, hear no evil, speak no evil.*

The night is lit by the dozen or so cop cars outside. Their lights flash in through the windows and fight with the soothing light of the living room. Tom paces, muttering to himself, hand pressed to his temple.

"Tom . . . coffee. Want a mug?" Dad says as if his thoughts and words refuse to align. He's better than Mom. She hasn't spoken. Tyler sits next to her, watching us, while she stares out the window into the black night.

Dad doesn't wait for his brother to reply. He pours two mugs, spilling some on the counter and not bothering to clean it up. When he places the mug into Tom's hands, the man finally stops pacing.

He's been here for a while, but only inside for the past half hour. He shuffled between the crime scene and the stupid reporters trying to get a look.

And now that the evidence has been bagged and the reporters are at a safe distance, he can talk. He just hasn't.

He sips his coffee and we all wait for him. "Sorry," he says. "There's just so much going on, I'm having trouble figuring out what to say."

"Well, what's the next step? What do we do now?" Tyler asks, and I'm glad he does, because none of us seem capable.

Tom stares into his coffee and then closes his eyes. "We process the evidence, which I guarantee belongs to Mary Matthison. And then we ask the neighbors if they've seen anything. But the entire town was just at the meeting." Tom lurches toward Dad. "You don't have a security system I'm not aware of, right? Cameras or anything like that?"

Dad shakes his head.

"Okay. We'll check with your neighbors, too. See if anyone on the street has one. We could catch a break that way."

Dad looks up from his coffee. "And if you don't?"

Tom sets down his mug. "There's the chance of fingerprints from the evidence, but since that hasn't been the case with the rest, it's unlikely." Tom looks over at me. His eyes are sunken in his face and ringed with dark circles. It's a terrifying image. "And now, since we have all of Mary back together, we're at the juncture we knew was coming."

"Are you saying what I think you're saying?" I ask.

"I am," Tom says.

I turn away, unable to form a response. For once, I don't know what to say. The lights keep flashing outside, red and blue, hypnotic. Tomorrow this will be all over the news, and combined with what was said about Calder and Matthison, this can't be good for me. How could they have done this when they were at the meeting? How could anyone have?

Dad stands in front of Tom. "But what's the plan, specifically? We understand that this maniac has it in for Avery, but what is he supposed to do? Dress like a girl for a day? A week? Longer? What if you never catch him and he never lets up?" Dad's voice gives out during his last question, as do his legs. He sits abruptly. Mom, who has turned her attention to us, starts crying.

Tom sits down next to his brother. "Gord, I'm not trying to upset you."

Dad raises his hand, cutting Tom off. "It's not me I'm worried about. Avery, come over, please."

I stand and Tom turns a chair for me to sit with them. I've sat with Dad and Tom like this a dozen times, easy, but there's a different weight to this man-to-man talk. It pins me to my chair, and I wait for one of them to begin.

"Av," Dad says, "what are you thinking? What do we do here?"

I feel strangely calm. But I think it's because I'm used to this scenario, and I'm letting this one settle in. It's about control. The killer has it, we don't, and so we have to do as we're told. Or else. This is the story of my life. People wanting to control who I am. Telling me I was just a tomboy, and later a lesbian, and now just playing a sick game with people. None of that is true. I am male. Simple. But people won't let it be, so it's not.

This killer has it in for me for this reason. That's obvious. I don't understand why he killed Mary, though. That part doesn't fit. But I guess there's no reason it should. This is his world and he can do whatever he wants. Must be nice.

"Tom, be honest with me for a minute, okay?" My voice is as calm as my thoughts, and I think Tom senses this because he doesn't get defensive.

"What do you want to know?"

"Do you have all of the evidence from Mary?"

Tom shifts in his seat. "Could you be more specific, Av?"

It is a vague question, so I clarify. "Do you have all of her?"

Tom tries to let the question slide off him. I can see it in the way he dips his head and looks away, but he's caught in it and has to answer. "No."

Dad gasps and out of the corner of my eye I see Tyler sit up.

Tom asks, "How did you know? Did he send you a text that you haven't told me about?"

I shake my head. "Just a feeling, I guess. Something's missing. There's a piece of her still out there, and it's everything. But he's going to make it hard for you to find. And he wants a distraction, a giant diversion from this case. Or he wants to see if I'll play along. And then reveal his secret to me."

Tom leans toward me. "How do you know this?"

"I don't. But everything about you is screaming that I'm right." I look him in his disheveled face. "Forensics is my thing. I've read more case files than probably you have. This guy isn't so different."

"Okay, then who is he? Why can't we catch a break, find any evidence that connects him?"

"Because he's better at hiding than you are at finding. He's good. And he knows it. And he wants to test all of us. The town, the cops, me. It's a game, for sure. And we can't lose. *I* refuse to lose."

"What does that mean?" Dad asks.

"It means I'll play along. I'll give him one day. Another if he wants it. And another. So long as that gets me closer to Mary, to what's left of her. I won't even ask you what that is."

Tom rubs his chin. "I don't know if I could even tell you, so thank you for not asking. And thank you for being willing to play this maniac's game."

"But, Tom," Dad starts.

"Gord, I won't let it go on any longer than it has to. That's disgusting. There will be an end point to this. We are not going allow this killer to dictate Avery's transition. He wants to meddle, fine. But he doesn't take over."

Tom turns back to me. "One day. Let's start with that. When do you think?"

"One day. But if shit gets weird, or he doesn't

take the bait that I've become, then we'll need to rethink."

"Agreed," Tom says. Both Mom and Dad nod. Tyler's staring into space.

"Obviously, he wants people to see me. When does school open, again?" I ask.

"I think I could convince the captain and your principal that we can open the doors on Monday."

Behind me I hear Tyler whisper, "Holy shit."

I turn in my seat, to Mom who is nearly lifeless. But I know she's listening, that she's grinding this through her brilliant mind. "What do you think?"

"I don't like it, but I don't think it's a mistake."

"Really, hon? You think this will help?" Dad asks.

She looks at him. "We're surrounded by cop cars. Your brother is dying from the stress of the case. This town is in an uproar. I don't see how this can hurt, except that it will make a spectacle out of our son." She draws back tears and turns to me. "But if you think you're strong enough to endure, I support you. I want this nightmare over, and I know you do, too. I'm just sorry that it's come to this."

That last statement was for Tom, but I feel pride in the rest of what she's said. I've been through so much shit, why not pile on some more. Can I endure? That's all I do.

I did nothing yesterday or today but stay hidden. I stayed in bed and watched stupid shit on TV, and did everything I could to ignore the news interruptions regarding the case. Of course I saw my house on TV from the night before, and listened to the reporters guess at what could have been left and why. And good for them, they managed to pull clips from me at the town hall going off on Calder and Matthison.

Besides hiding, I waited. Waited for a text or a call from Beth or from Charlie. I didn't get anything from either. I don't really know if I'll be able to forgive them after this if they continue to leave me high and dry. Especially if I get no support tomorrow. School starts again. Mom's already bought my outfit.

She brought it in while I was sleeping and put it on my desk chair. I awoke and thought someone was standing in my room. But no, it was just a vestige of myself. One I thought I had left behind.

I ignore the dress now and zip up my coat. I did make one request of Tom, and he's paying it back, now.

"You sure?" he asks, when I come down the stairs.

I answer by walking out the front door and into the night, straight past Officer Howard and to Tom's cruiser. I hop in shotgun and he gets behind the wheel.

We don't speak. He drives and I think. I won't waste any words on him. All of my energy is being saved for Mary.

Tom's headlights illuminate the marble head-stones as we make our way down the cemetery road. It's eerie but still too bright. When we reach Mary's grave I tell Tom to kill the lights.

"But how will you see?"

I open the door and see just fine. The rumor is that the Matthisons intend to have an enormous tombstone created, a white angel hovering above where Mary has been laid to rest. Now, it's just a simple stone, marking where the angel will be. I stand before her and don't know how to proceed. The ground around her plot has hardened in the cold. It's lumpy, disturbed, not at all peaceful looking. And how could it be with her killer still on the loose?

I run my hand along the stone and think of the angel's wings that will rise above here. Mary loved talking about angels when we were kids. "They serve God, just like we do," she said. I had no clue what she was talking about.

"When we pray, God hears us. Sometimes He sends angels to help, either to show us something or to share a message."

I loved the idea that these winged spectral crea-tures could descend from above and help us with our needs. I began praying for one to help me, even though I had no faith. I never told Mary that. But somehow, I think she knew.

I lie on the ground and turn my face into the cold stone marker. It feels good, comforting. I haven't been this close to Mary in years. And in spite of my bravery, last night, I'm nervous, now, and need her advice.

"What should I do?" I ask. "If I do what he says, then he has control. Then we're playing his game. Is that the smart move or just stupidity?"

I think of Tom and how fearful he is of the killer's knowledge and of how much of this is all in his hands. I lie on the cold ground, feeling the wind cut through me, but not caring. It's not that I expect an answer. This isn't some psychic attempt. But there's no one I'd rather ask, and if it has to be this way, so be it.

"If you were here, what would you tell me to do?" I run my fingertip over the stone. "Would you have me tell them to fuck off?" I smile because Mary never swore. "Would you help me pick out an outfit? Would you help me with my hair and my makeup?" The tears are sliding, but I can still talk. Emotion hasn't overtaken me yet.

"If I walked into school tomorrow wearing a dress, would you hold my hand? Would you tell me that everything is going to be all right?" I wipe away the tears. "Or would you tell me to run, to be afraid, to never look back? Just like we had to that day?"

The wind lifts and I huddle closer. "He's a monster, your dad. The reverend. I know you told me. I saw what I saw, too. But like you said, no one cares. No one ever will, because he's mightier than all of us."

"I think Calder might be just like him, too. And I get why you were with him now. Not because you wanted to. That never really seemed possible. No, because your dad wanted you to. And I bet it saved you from things. From beatings. But look where it got you."

A sob racks me and I have to wait until it passes, until I can speak again. Because I'm not done yet.

"But I don't know if it's either of them. How could it be? I do know it's not the poor hunter who found your body. He's not working with some accomplice. This is an issue of pure hatred. Against you. Against me. Who the fuck hated us this much? And why?"

I take a deep breath, filling my lungs with the searing cold, and I let it out in a stream of mist. "He's so close, Mary. Did you know him? Did you sense he was coming? Because I feel him everywhere. Like he's always watching." I reach up to where I imagine the tip of the angel's wing will be.

"I hope you have angels with you now. I hope they're doing God's work and I hope they still listen. Because I'm praying to you, to them, to God if He exists, to anyone who will listen. Please help me."

❖

I wake early, before my alarm clock, and when I see the dress, I don't startle. It's not some vestige from my past. It's me, in this moment, in this horrendous nightmare that won't end, understanding that I have to do what I have to do, and that's rip myself out of where I am in my transition and put myself back into a shell that will never fit, regardless of how many times I'm told it looks good on me.

My stomach flips, but I manage to drink coffee. At least I'll be wide awake for this. After coffee I get in the shower and lather, rinse, repeat and then grab my razor. Fortunately, I guess, I'm not at the wiry, man-hair stage of my transition yet. I know it takes time for some, and possibly this is the one moment of grace I'll receive today, because I've never shaved my chest. I have always wanted hair I could expose. But now, like the gentle stubble on my face, and the slightly longer hair under my arms, my chest hair falls prey to the razor. In a few minutes I've wiped away what testosterone has taken months to create.

It's easier shaving my legs, because I've done this before, albeit reluctantly. I burn through two razors on my left leg. Another two on my right, and I'm disgustingly smooth. Tears well up, but I hold them in. I'd better practice now, because once I leave, there's no telling how awful today is going to be.

My parents and Tom met with my principal yesterday to discuss what is going down. From what they told me, he wasn't thrilled with the idea, because he can envision how much of a distraction this will be. But he also realizes that everyone in town is aware of the demand, and will understand that I'm not trying to create more drama. Ultimately, he's sorry that I have to suffer.

And suffer I will.

Back in my room I dry off and put on my one layer of dignity: boxer briefs, not panties. But a bra waits for me. My binder sits forgotten on my desk. I fight back tears again.

Then there's a knock on my door. I cover up by instinct, as Mom comes in. She sees me, the position I'm in and opens her arms, enveloping me in an enormous hug. Her tears flow as freely as the water from the shower. And we stay like this for a moment, mother and son, but not looking at all like that from the outside.

Mom dries her tears and then holds my shoulders. "We're going to get through today. Your father and I will be at school in an instant, if you need us."

"Thanks, Mom." I can't risk any more. I hand her the bra and turn my back to her. She understands. I slide my arms through and she clasps the back.

"Too tight?"

I wiggle my shoulders, testing the elasticity. "It's good."

Mom moves to the chair and grabs the very plain cotton dress that she picked up. She drops it to the floor and I remember enough to step in and hike up. She takes it from there and zips up the back. It's not nearly as tight as my binder, but once it's up, I feel momentarily breathless.

I slide into the light sweater and flats she has laid out and then sit at my desk and wait for her to do what she can with my hair. I've kept it relatively short for years. Like Bieber length, so there's not much, but possibly just enough. She brushes and combs and teases and twists. Fifteen minutes later she says "there," and in spite of how helpful she's being, how much I know this hurts her, I want to hit her for how thrilled she sounded over her achievement with my hair. But I rein myself in. The one thing I am expert at, because I know it's not about her, and she's not about making me feel awful. This is about survival.

Dad drives and Tyler comes with us and I try my hardest not to catch glimpses of myself in the rearview mirror, but it's like a car accident, I have to look.

I'll give Mom credit, I look very much like the picture the killer sent, ugly pigtails and all. Tyler is doing his best not to, but he keeps staring. His poor brain is probably more scrambled than my own.

"No Beth? No Charlie?" he asks.

"No, it's safer for them this way."

Which is a lie so bold I'm surprised he doesn't call me out on it. There are four cop cars escorting us today. If anyone were to try anything, they'd need a hell of a lot of luck getting through this motorcade.

We pass the cluster of news vans that have been parked out front of school for over a week now. The cameras move like sunflowers, following us. I hold my breath and we enter the school parking lot.

"Shit," Dad says, and we all look to see what he's talking about. It doesn't take long.

The flock is out front, their ranks seeming to have multiplied. They hold hands and sing and pray. And wait. For me.

Dad parks and turns around. "You okay?"

I shake my head and the pigtails flop about.

"Makes sense." He pats my knee, and it's skin on skin, which is so weird. We both look up with the same face. And we laugh, which is absurd, but we laugh and so do Mom and Tyler, and I think for one brief moment that I can laugh my way through this. Then I step out of the car and in between Officer Howard and the other three cops. I feel like the girl from the famous integration painting. And I feel as scared as she looked.

"Call us, Avery. The first second you need help," Dad says.

"Good luck, man," Tyler says, and then they fade from me, into the distance, as I walk, surrounded by officers, toward the flock.

They have stopped praying and are staring, slack-jawed and eyes unblinking.

Calder looks at me and smiles so wide I feel like vomiting. Eva disbands from the group and comes to me.

"Avery! You are just adorable." She looks back to the flock. "You see her?" They nod like a line of lobotomized bobbleheads.

"I'm still male, Eva. It's *he*."

"Well, not today it isn't." She puts a hand to her cheek and looks me over from head to toe. I feel like one of her prized animals, not even close to human anymore. "Lord, Mary's heart would be full today."

"What?" I don't even know how I ask, my mouth is so dry.

"She always used to say how adorable you were growing up, and how she bet you still would be if you stopped with the tomboy routine."

"No. She didn't. Mary knew me better than that."

All heads snap at the mention of her name or at my vehement denial. Eva leans in. "You keep telling yourself that."

Tom joins the ranks of my escort and we move along.

"Anything yet?" Tom asks.

I stare at him, hoping he sees the absolute hatred I feel for everyone and everything in this moment, including him. I reach into my purse, because I have a purse, because for today that's what I use, a purse for my phone. Nothing. I shake my head. "Not yet."

"All right. It's early though. I hoped he would text and let you off the hook as soon as you arrived."

"Why would you think that?"

"Wishful thinking, Avery. Or just plain old hope."

I like that's he's hopeful, but I also think it's sad that it's come to this for him to feel that way. I swallow the shame and walk on, into a day I never thought I'd have to endure, again.

Principal Williams meets up with my entourage as soon as we enter.

"Sorry," he says and seems as if he's trying not to stare at me. "I was caught on the phone with a reporter." He looks at me now. "How are you, Avery?"

"I'm great. Best day ever." I want to fist pump to punctuate the sarcasm, but I know that's not going to help anything.

"Right, of course," he says and turns back to Tom. "What's the plan?"

"It's a waiting game." Tom shoots me a look. "Like I said yesterday, we need to see what he's going to do."

"Right. I know. And you think we're still safe. I have so many other students to consider."

Tom turns so he's closer to Williams, but not so close I can't hear him. "Again, let me remind you of our conversation. If we had any reason to believe there was a threat to the school, this building wouldn't even be open. The threat is all on Avery."

They both look at me, and I give them a thumbs-up.

"I know, Tom. I'm sorry. I'm just nervous for us all."

The first bell rings and I leave Tom with Principal Williams. I'm off to class, now with Officer Howard and another cop at my side.

I think most rational people would recognize the fact that today's not quite a typical school day, what with the cops and the death threats and all, and yeah, the kids in the hall do, but not in the serious way I think my principal and Tom are expecting.

"Oh shit! Let me get a selfie!" And they rush in and try for an angle that gets them with me and the cops. Me with my pigtails, either looking away or flipping off the phone. It's complete bullshit. But no one's stopping it. This feels so much like it did when I first started dressing in boy clothes, and insisted the school consider me as such. Which meant issues with the bathroom and PE and even stupid classroom activities like "boys on this side, girls on the other." It was a clusterfuck then because it was new and confusing. It's a clusterfuck now because they all get to behave as they truly see me without fear of getting in trouble. To them, I'm a joke.

We make it to class and one officer peels off and stands at the door, while Officer Howard comes into class. He stands in the back and blends as well as any fully armed police officer in a high school can.

My English teacher steps around the other officer and tiptoes into class. She sees me and an awkward moment ensues. She says nothing, but her body screams everything, as she makes a beeline to her desk. The class bubbles with laughter, and I clench as many muscles as I can to fight the urge to scream.

The bell rings and my teacher turns, composed and more like herself. "Okay, okay, easy everyone." She looks at me, like she might a new student. It seems as if she's contemplating asking me to say a few words about myself. I've never had an issue with her before, and think she's a decent human being, which is more than I can say for some of the teachers here. But her full-body scan has me unnerved.

"I know it's been a difficult time for all of you, and so instead of reading the short story I had planned, we're going to watch the movie version."

The class is pumped, and attention is immediately diverted away from me. I say a silent "thank you." But then the lights go off and once the movie begins, I hear whispers. Just loud enough:

I think she looks beautiful.

Like Emma Watson hot.

I think I'd do her. Does that make me gay?

No. It makes you straight. Of course it makes you gay. Av's a dude.

No, he's not. She has a snatch.

Heads turn and consider me in the dim light. Up until now, unless these kids went to school with me in grade school, they might not actually know what is up. Which is both comforting, and at the same time harrowing. People have always talked shit, but this, this shows a complete level of ignorance I never knew existed. Or I simply ignored.

When class ends it's obvious a tide has turned. Kids are glancing at phones and then sweeping the halls, looking. It's as if they're on a scavenger hunt. They are. And they've found me.

"Avery! So adorable!" This from a girl so gorgeous it's disarming. Because of this, my escort has stopped, which provides an opportunity for the girl to snap a selfie with me. She then looks at the image and squeals with delight, before moving on as if I wasn't even there. Others surge forward.

"Avery! Let's go out!" Some kid has flowers and is thrusting them at me. I've never seen him before. But I guarantee he'll get his five minutes of YouTube fame.

We're packed in by a wall of students surrounding us, but the cops know what to do. They take out their billy clubs and hold them in front of their bodies, and they push.

"Clear out!" Howard screams. "We can and will arrest you."

Through the wall of protection, kids laugh and hold phones steady. I am going to be everywhere online, and I realize just how much of this is precisely what the killer wants. Repentance by humiliation. The price had better be worth it.

The loudspeaker thrums to life. "Students! Get to your classes now. Anyone caught in the halls after the second bell will be suspended!" Most kids move along, but some laugh and take more pictures. At least they respected Mary more. I never expected similar treatment, but I wish they could remember who I'm doing this for.

Mrs. Luce greets me at the door and looks only at my face, as if she's refusing to see what's in front of her. "Are you okay?"

She's genuine. I can feel the emotion in her voice.

"I'll be a lot better when today is over," I say.

She nods. "Thank you, Avery."

I take my seat, and it's the same as in English class. Kids talk shit, take pictures, and I try to stay as stoic as possible. The worst part is, I looked for Charlie when I sat. Maybe it's better that he's not here. Because what if he didn't stick up for me?

Then Luce turns on a *Forensics Files* episode to kill the class. It's one I've seen before, but that's fine, it's gory and mysterious.

But as the stories unfold, the class stirs and I hear Mary's name. Then this: *I hope he's taken more pieces of Mary, because if he keeps torturing Avery with them, we'll never have school again.*

The kid turns, as stupid kids will do, just to see if they've been heard. He has, by Luce and by me. She and I exchange a glance and then I look at the kid. He ducks his head between his shoulders and laughs to his friend. Luce shakes her head and turns, and when she does, the asshole and his friend both stare at me. The asshole's friend mimes whipping out his dick and having it chopped off. He pretends to throw it to me. "Here, it's as close as you're going to get to the real thing."

All the control it has taken to get me into this outfit, into this school, and through this morning falls away in an instant. I bolt from my desk, charge up the aisle, and punch the dick-throwing kid in the jaw.

His head wobbles to the side and when he rights, I punch him in the eye, and then the mouth, and then the other eye. Just as I land a straight shot to his nose, the lights come on and Luce is at the switch, and Officer Howard is pinning my arms behind my back.

The class is bubbling over, looking at the kid whose ass I just kicked. I'm about to defend myself, to scream about what he just said, but some guy next to me yells, "Look at her nip-ons!" And since I can't get out from under Officer Howard's vice grip, all I can do is look down at myself. I'm covered in the kid's blood, and indeed, my nipples are at stiff attention.

❖

"This is all my fault. I don't know why I thought it would work." Tom paces the length of Principal Williams's office, and I agree with every word.

"You did what you had to," my principal says, sounding very much like he's trying to help a despondent student. "There must be some silver lining in this, some way that this has helped your case." He looks between Tom and me.

I hold up my bloodied hands. "Yeah, a real step forward today."

Both men look at me and I hate them. I reach up and pull out the pigtails and then run my hand through my hair. It's wild and crazy and just how I like it.

"Avery, you can't. He hasn't texted you." Tom is at my side, trying to figure out how to put me back together. But puzzles aren't really his strong suit.

"I can. And I just did. And if the psycho out there has a problem with it, why do I give a shit? This," I say, pointing at myself, "was to help you. To buy you some time. Well, I've given you a morning, and now I'm done."

Tom goes to answer but my parents burst through the door. Dad rushes at his brother, demanding to know why he didn't call sooner.

Mom comes to my side and picks up my hand, bandaged by the nurse, but still oozing blood. She looks at my hair, and has to see the blood spatter across my dress. She smiles. "Good for you."

I stand and she rubs my back, and we move toward the door.

"Wait, where are you going? We have to talk about this," Tom says, ignoring my father.

Principal Williams stands as well. "Yes, we need to figure out what to do here."

Mom leans across the principal's desk. "How about you suspend the kid who provoked this." Williams goes to answer but Mom puts up her hand. "Don't you dare go there. You think I don't know how to use a phone? All morning kids have been taunting Avery. If he snapped, that's your fault, not his. Figure out your own problems, and we'll take care of ours."

"But we share this problem," Tom says.

"Yeah. And your solution sucked," Dad says. "We're leaving." He turns to Principal Williams. "Make this right or you will hear from our lawyer. The evidence is everywhere."

Dad's words bolster me, and I hold my head high as we exit. Yet, what he said about the evidence, I know he wasn't implying anything, but it's got me thinking.

Tom follows us into the hall. "Avery, just a second."

Mom and Dad look at me, seeing if I want to address him. I do. "Don't worry, Tom, I'll let you know when he texts."

"I know you will." He pauses. "Look at me. Please, Avery."

It's not his words but the desperation in his voice that compels me to do what he wants. He looks worse than the kid I beat up. His eyes are bloodshot and ringed with dark circles. His skin is gray, and his stubble isn't even remotely groomed. He's a man at the end of his rope.

"I am sorry for what happened. I wanted this to work. I wanted to buy some time. And stupidly, I did that without thinking of how this would affect you. I fucked up." His tears are more than I can bear.

I go to him, hug him tight, and say, "Then make it right."

He squeezes me and whispers, "I promise."

The only sound that breaks the silence of the ride home is Tyler opening and closing the door. He looks me over, like so many have today, but with infinitely more compassion. He takes out his phone and scrolls through his accounts. They're all pictures or videos of me. I nod and he puts his phone away. We sit and my mind runs through all that just occurred. I don't feel the slightest bit of remorse for having beaten up that kid. I only wish Charlie had been there to see it.

He and Beth were nowhere to be seen, though. I have to assume a whole lot about what that implies, but not now. First, I need to get out of these clothes and back to myself.

My phone chimes and my entire family turns. Dad drifts in the lane and then pulls the car over. I read the text aloud to them.

Well, you've been a bad girl. You need to ask forgiveness for your sins.

"Avery, don't reply. Let me call Tom," Dad says, but I'm already typing.

Why? What good will that do me? Are you going to reveal yourself?

No. If you find me, you find me. But so far your uncle isn't good at that. You need to ask Him for forgiveness, and if you do, then maybe I will show you some mercy.

Why should I trust you?

Why trust anyone? Because you believe.

"Read what he's written," Dad is holding out the phone so Tom can hear. I read the exchange, and then Tom starts talking, but I ignore him.

I believe. I believe I will find you. And I know I will never ask for forgiveness.

Okay. Game on.

My parents promptly lose their shit over my response, as does Tom when Dad reads it to him, but I don't care anymore. This has to end, and if I'm the one to do it, so be it. I'm done hiding, and I'm done being someone else's plaything.

We get home and it has become normal now to have two officers flank our every step. So normal that we argue all the way inside, in spite of their presence. I charge up to my room and sit at my desk. I light a cigar and prepare to dive into the virtual world I know so well.

Outside my door, Dad yells, "At least open a window!" He's not going any further than that, so I do him the favor and enjoy how the cool air snaps me awake.

I sift through blog posts and case studies and long, academic papers about decomposition and insects and larvae. I watch as many YouTube clips as I can from the Body Farm. I stuff it all in, hoping that once it's there, it will churn and a shred of something useful will pop out. Until then, my brain just hurts, and I can no longer push away the image of Mary's disfigured face every time I see a dead body.

I head downstairs in a haze, calmer than before and feeling a world better in my regular clothes. My phone chimes, and fortunately my parents are busy cooking dinner and too busy to hear.

It's Charlie. *I saw what happened, Av. Holy shit am I sorry.*

I resist saying anything I'll regret. *Why weren't you there?*

Dad wouldn't let me go. Back at work with him, again. He just gave me my phone back.

So is this when you tell me how right you are? Or, how wrong I was?

The text bubble emerges, and Ty comes into the living room. "Who's that?" he asks, eyeing my phone like I'm holding a gun.

"Charlie."

"Good. Tell him to get his ass back to school. You need someone."

His words strike me as both accurate and pathetic. I do need someone, but mostly I need myself.

It's not like that, Av. How did it go? Did you hear anything?

I heard lots of shit. But you mean from the psycho you're scared of? Oh, yeah. We've got a date.

Avery, I'm sorry.

I don't bother replying, because he can apologize all he wants, but until he does something, it's all hollow. At least Beth had the courage to say what she felt and the conviction to see it through. I've had absolutely no communication with her since she laid into me on her porch.

The door opens and I look up. We're all here, so either Officer Howard has to piss, or we have a visitor who has chosen not to ring the doorbell.

Tom walks down the hall. I notice this, that he walks, doesn't swagger. He's lost that along the way.

He sees me and stops, puts a hand to his mouth and pulls down, as if trying to dispel whatever he's mumbling to himself.

"Just tell me," I say. I'm done with all pretense.

He comes to me, grabs my shoulder, bending my ear toward him. "It's Beth. She's in the hospital."

"What happened?" My voice sounds out of body, echoing back.

"Someone attacked her at her house today. She wasn't in school, and so it didn't come to my attention earlier."

"Is she all right? Who was it?"

Tom squeezes tighter. "She's fine, she was just knocked unconscious."

"What do you mean *just*?"

"Fortunately, he only knocked her out and left it at that."

I close my eyes and picture Beth, lying on the ground. It's a disturbing image, and one too close to what I assume must have happened to Mary. "Okay. What else?"

"Why did you think there's more?"

I open my eyes and they feel as dead as I do inside. "Really? Like this is some coincidence? Tell me."

Tom looks around the house. Ty's back in his room and my parents are still in the kitchen. Right now it's just the two of us. It won't be for long.

"The scripture left in Mary's mouth, the one written on the reverend's paper . . ."

My body tenses at every word.

"There was scripture, written on the reverend's paper, pinned to Beth."

My jaw crunches my back teeth. I want them turned to dust. "And?"

Tom clears his throat. "I've memorized it. Luke 13:3—'I tell you, Nay: but, except ye repent, ye shall all likewise perish.'"

I will myself to not fall apart. I am already to blame for Mary's death. I will not be able to live with myself if I am responsible for another.

Beth's hospital room is as guarded as my home. The officers allow me inside and her parents are the first to see me. They share a look of trepidation and then anger. They were right, and they know it, and I know it. But that doesn't change anything.

"Avery, hey," she says, turning slowly toward me.

Beth's parents look at her and then the monitors that surround her. All seems steady. "Please," she says, and they squeeze her hands and then walk past me, wordlessly.

I pull up a chair beside her and hold her hand. It's warm and soft and takes me back. "I'm so sorry," I say.

"Not your fault." Her voice is almost as bruised as her skull, and I wish I could heal both.

"Still, I am sorry, Beth. You were right. Or your parents were. We're all in danger. But did you see him?"

"Yes. He had a mask on, so I didn't see his face, just his size. He's big, Av." Her eyes glaze over and I worry about what this will do to her, long term. "I ran, but he hit me in the back of the head. I remember that. The pain at the back of my head, and then nothing. Black." Her lips tremble as she finishes. "It was horrifying, Av. I thought I was going to die. Even worse, I thought I would end up like Mary."

No one, not even Tom has suggested this, but we all know it's true. If this is the same guy, then, for whatever reason, Beth was saved. I squeeze her hand tighter.

"You've got to be smart, Av. Stay safe." Saying this causes her discomfort, but she smiles through it. "Please tell me you're not going back to school."

"How did you hear?"

She looks toward the hall. "It's not just the kids at school who are watching those clips. The staff here is all about what's going on."

"So you saw?"

"That wasn't you, Avery. That was someone forced to play dress-up."

I press my head against her bed. The starch emanates a clean so unnatural, I sit back up. "It was horrible, and no, I'm not going back. Not that I think I can. Not until this is over. Which, fortunately, may be helped by today. There were footprints on your porch. Fibers from the note. It's not a breakthrough, but it's something they can work with."

Beth rubs the top of my head, her IV tube trailing along my ear. "Well, I'm glad my near-death has been helpful." She tries to force a smile, but I shake my head at her.

"Don't. You are lucky to be alive. I am lucky, because if he . . . if he . . ." I can't finish, but the tears that slide down Beth's cheeks tell me I don't have to.

"I know, Av. But we've got to be careful, and you need to keep doing what's right. It's brave what you did today. I've never thought anything less of you."

I kiss her hand. "You should rest. I think you're starting to hallucinate."

She laughs and then winces, and I feel bad for hurting her. "I'm serious, though, Av. You're brave, but please be smart."

"How so. Have you heard what he wants now?"

"No." Her voice sounds like she's almost asleep.

I hesitate to go on, but I can see in her eyes she wants me to. "Go to church. Ask for forgiveness. I'm guessing like confession or something."

She looks away. "Or else?"

"Did they tell you what the note pinned to you said?"

"Yeah."

I put my hands together, as if in prayer. "That's my guess."

More tears flow now, and I find a tissue and wipe them away. And then I stay, hovering over her. "What should I do?" I ask.

"Just do it. If it ends this . . ."

"But I don't know if it will."

"Of course you don't, but that's not the point. Would you do this if it were Mary asking?" She closes her eyes and in a moment she is breathing heavily, asleep, and I'll bet, fully aware of how I would have answered.

I step into the hall and look for Beth's parents. I don't see them so I turn to one of the cops at the door. I almost stop myself from speaking, because it's Officer Wright. "She's asleep. Let them know when they come back."

He doesn't reply, just stares at me.

"Did you hear me?" I ask.

"Yeah, I heard you." He works his jaw when he finishes, and my instincts tell me to keep going, that I'm riled from having seen how bad Beth is, but that other part keeps me in place.

"Is there a problem?"

Wright looks me over, just like the kids at school today. "Yeah, there are lots of problems."

"And let me guess, you believe that they would all be solved by one easy solution."

He smiles, large and smarmy under his mustache. "Avery, if you did us all the favor of no longer existing, I would be a much happier man."

I smile back. "Exactly my sentiments about you." I walk away before he has a chance to reply or I have the opportunity to do anything else.

Tom is in the waiting room where I left him. He stands when he sees me. "How is she?"

"Tired. But she seems all right. Her parents didn't threaten to kill me, so I'm guessing she's getting better."

Tom nods and puffs his cheeks. "Yeah, they're pissed, but we're doing everything we can."

"Any idea? She saw him, just not his face. And you've got some evidence now. What about the neighbors?"

Tom looks around. "It helps, trust me. It's more than we've had so far. We're following up with the neighbors, but nothing, yet. I think he parked a street over and walked in. That's why we have the footprint, but no one saw a car."

"The fibers? Anything else?"

"That takes time. You know that. Forensics can be slow. But they're at the top of the list. Hopefully we'll know something by the morning."

I look back down the hall, not trying to think about Wright, but his words strike me. "Was this meant as a warning or did he try to kill her?"

Tom pulls at his face. "Tough to answer. A head shot like that, you can't know the outcome. I think he was prepared for either scenario, but that note makes me think he wanted Beth to live."

I shake involuntarily. And Tom grabs my shoulder.

"Sorry, Av. I'm just trying to be straight with you."

"I know," I say, in spite of my clattering teeth.

"Come on, let's get you out of here."

We head toward the door, but I stop.

"Something wrong, Av?"

"No. Yeah. Maybe. Just to be straight with you, Wright talked shit again."

"Not surprised. He's got his own holy-roller shit that I have no time for."

"I thought you said he's good at his job."

Tom's nostrils flare. "Trust me, I wouldn't let anyone near Beth who isn't up to snuff. All right?"

I nod, but I don't want to. He's part of the flock, I get it. He'll do his job, and do it well, but that doesn't mean he has to respect the people he helps.

"Whatever happened to the God and love and peace believers?" I ask.

"I think they're just a figment of our imagination, Av."

I plop onto the couch next to Tyler when I get home. My parents go see Tom at the door.

"How is she?" he asks.

"Not good. He hit her so hard it bruised her skull."

"What the fuck?" Ty rubs the back of his head. "Did she see him? Can she ID who it was?"

"No. Asshole wore a mask."

Tyler stares into space, the show he's watching no longer relevant. "Don't let this eat at you, Av. It's not your fault."

"Well, it's kind of my fault. Just like I'm kind of the reason Mary's dead."

Tyler spins around on the cushion to face me. "Don't say that. It's not. You didn't kill Mary, that psycho did."

"I know. But even when he's caught, his motivation is going to be full of my name."

We both sit for a moment, the noise from the TV and the sound of Tom and my parents' conversation down the hall filling the space.

"You ever think about killing yourself, Av?"

My skin prickles. "What did you say?"

"You heard me. I was online, reading something about the case, and there was this link to an article about transgender kids and the suicide rates. They're like sky high."

I know the stats, something like 41 percent of us try to kill ourselves. And that's those of us who are out about our transition. I can't even imagine the number if it included those who were still in the closet.

"They are, Ty. We talk about that at PFLAG. You know, numbers to call, things you should do if we get feeling that way."

"Okay. Okay, good," he says. "So you promise."

I shift in my seat. "I promise to reach out if my mind goes *there*."

"No, you have to promise not to do it."

Ty's looking at me now, that mature part of him fighting with the still naive side that believes just because you say it, then it's true.

"I can't promise that, Ty."

"Why?" His question is almost a cry.

"Because I want to be honest with you. My life here with you guys is great. But I think you've got a sense how the rest of the world sees me. If they ever get a chance to fuck up my head enough . . ." I stare into his eyes. "Well, I just don't know."

He lurches toward me and holds me tight. I can hear his tears gurgling along my neck. "You look past that shit, Av. You look past it all and you remember us. You remember Mary."

I hug him back and promise that I will, and hope with all that I am that I'm able to keep it.

Our moment is broken by yelling outside our door. It sounds like, "Is he here?"

Dad and Mom rush down the hallway and sit with us. "Tom's on it," Dad says, and the door opens. The man's voice grows louder.

"Is he here? Is my son here? Charlie?"

I bounce off the couch and head to the door. My family is at my heels. Charlie's dad is in the driveway, looking every direction but at Tom who's trying to talk to him.

"There you are!" He points at me. "Where is he? Where is Charlie?"

Tom turns and sees me and appears relieved, as if possibly I can help. He doesn't know how wrong he is.

"I haven't seen him, Mr. McCarthy. I thought he was at work with you."

"He was, but I went to get dinner and when I came home he was gone."

"I just got back from the hospital, but my parents have been here." I turn to them, now on the steps. "Have you seen Charlie?"

They shake their heads and come down the steps, into the driveway.

"What seems to be going on, Seamus?" Dad uses Charlie's dad's first name and it feels weird.

Mr. McCarthy rears back, looking horrified. "Don't come near me. You and your family and the fucking freak! My son's missing, and I guarantee it's because of your abomination!"

Dad clenches his fists and I am blown away by Mr. McCarthy's anger. He's always been quiet and questioning, but never mean. This, this must be what Charlie meant.

"I'm going to have to ask you to get off my property, Seamus. If not, Tom will arrest you. I wish I knew where Charlie is, but maybe he went out and forgot to tell you."

Mr. McCarthy grabs his own hair so hard it has to hurt. "He didn't! You don't understand. Your girl, boy, whatever, he's Charlie's only friend. He's always been odd, just like his mother. But ever since she passed . . ." He can't go on. Mr. McCarthy looks down. "He's all I've got. And I swear to you, he's been taken." Then he looks up and directly at me. "And you're to blame."

My stomach drops with the sickening realization of not only Charlie's home life, but that his twisted father is right. Mary. Beth. Now Charlie. I am the common bond.

"Tom, get on this. Charlie's gone," I say.

Tom seems at a loss for which direction to take. "You're sure. Because if I call this in, it's going to take away men from our hunt for whoever went after Beth."

"Listen to yourself, Tom. It's the same person. Whoever got Beth, has Charlie. And killed Mary. I'd bet my life on it."

CHAPTER 21

We drive and we search, because there's nothing else to do. Tom gathered his men, got a recent picture of Charlie to all of them and sent them out. They took Mr. McCarthy home and began there, just in case Charlie was in the shower or the basement, or had actually gone out like we all hoped. He wasn't and he didn't.

So now, with Officer Howard behind me, we swing around the neighborhood, hoping to see him burning off steam, taking a walk, drinking a beer in the park, something. Anything but what we're fearing.

I watch Howard's sweeping light, careful to be on the lookout for Charlie dodging it. Or, if not Charlie, someone else. But while I do, I cannot erase what just transpired with Charlie's dad. Seeing Mr. McCarthy drove home how awful it must be for Charlie. His mom is dead and his father seems like another raging asshole. He called me an *abomination*.

It's awful to know how Charlie's own father thinks about him. What if he were my dad? There's no way in hell I'd still be alive. Beth and Charlie were right, my parents are truly outstanding. That's really not the most comforting thought though, because that means the more accepted way is to behave like Mr. McCarthy. Rage and hatred are the norm? Since when?

We drive through downtown, past school, and toward the outskirts. The woods lie heavy and dense in the dark. In spite of the falling leaves, the town is shrouded by them. So many homes and lives kept in the dark.

We head up the hill, back toward my house, and on the right is the reverend's church. It is shut up tight and looks downright adorable with its enormous wooden doors and high-pitched roof. The walls are adorned only with the stained-glass windows embedded. It's a simple building, for a simple understanding of the world. Good and Bad. Right and Wrong. Saint and Sinner.

There's a light on inside, a flickering candle it seems, or just my imagination. I stop my car, and Howard locks it up behind me. I see him in my mirror, looking pissed. I signal toward the church and pull into the parking lot.

The light is clear now. It wasn't me seeing things. I know it's just one of the candles they use for prayers for people. You put in a dollar, light a big, glass-enclosed candle, kneel and say a prayer and hope for the best. I kind of want to go and light one for Beth. And one for Charlie.

Officer Howard rolls up to my window, his passenger side down. "What's up?" he says.

"Just the candle. It caught my attention."

Howard looks at the window, nods, looks back at me.

And why wouldn't there be? When Mary went missing the church looked like it was on fire, with all the flames that were burning in hope of her safe return. They've been burning since, for a capture.

But tonight there's just the one as far as I can tell. Why have they stopped praying?

A chill like I haven't felt since I was a child slides under my skin, rides up my arm and grips my temple.

"Officer Howard?"

"Yeah?"

"How come there's only one lit? Haven't they all been burning ever since Mary disappeared?"

His face brightens as if he were before the flame. "No shit?" He opens his door and then turns to me. "Stay here. Do not get out!"

His walkie-talkie echoes off the side of the building as he tells dispatch where he's headed. I wonder if he has a key or some way of getting in. Do they just keep the doors unlocked? If so, that's faith.

His flashlight illuminates from within, casting the stained glass in a harsh, false light, ruining its appearance. The light bobs around, and then I hear Officer Howard talking rapid fire. Charlie's name is mentioned three or four times, and I know he's in there.

I don't think, I get out of my car and I run to the door. It's been latched open.

"Charlie, Charlie, can you hear me?" Officer Howard's voice echoes off the stone within.

I follow the sound and find him, leaning over Charlie, who is unconscious, or worse. His arms are spread to his side, and he's been placed on the floor against the prayer candles. A piece of paper is pinned to his chest.

"You can't be here," Officer Howard says.

"I can't be a lot of things," I say, then I lean close. "Charlie! You wake up right fucking now!" I smack him so hard my hand throbs. But Charlie's eyes flutter and then open and then he sees us.

Howard starts screaming into his walkie-talkie, saying that Charlie is alive.

And then I notice the cuts on his palms, the ring of blood around his head, and because of this I look at his feet. Sure enough, they're bloodied, as is his side.

"Charlie," I say, and he looks at me, the whites of his eyes so bright in the dark. The rest of him is covered in shadow.

"Help me, Av," he says, and I see that his hands are bound to the frame.

I untie one hand and Howard joins in and undoes the other. Charlie rubs his wrist and the paper on his chest flutters. Howard goes to unpin it but Charlie grabs it first. "The fuck?" he says and reads. He closes his eyes when he's finished and hands it off. I let Howard take it, but read over his shoulder.

Revelation 2:5—Remember therefore from whence thou art fallen, and repent, and do the first works; or else I will come unto thee quickly, and will remove thy candlestick out of his place, except thou repent.

For now, I ignore the scripture, ignore the fact that it is, like with Mary, and like with Beth, from Matthison's supply. I focus on Charlie, because I know the cops are coming, and an ambulance, and probably his rage-fueled father.

"Do you remember anything? Did you see who it was?"

Charlie shakes his head. "No. They wore masks and then they put a cloak or a bag or something over my head. And then tied me up. But one was big and one was small."

"Where?"

"At my house." Charlie's eyes go wide with the memory. "Then they must have hit me and knocked me out, because I remember waking up here, still tied up. They'd put that crown on my head and had already cut me up." He stills and looks at me. "They didn't speak. Not a word. It's almost as if they weren't real."

"But there were two?" Howard leans in and asks. "You're sure."

Charlie looks at the floor and back inside his memory. "Yeah, it was definitely two. I saw them at the door and was confused."

"Is there anything else, anything you can think of, right now that we should know?" Officer Howard asks.

Charlie shakes his head. "They did speak. Well, the big one did. At the house. He said this was for Avery."

I feel like knocking all the candles over and burning this place down. Even though I knew this was the reason, it hurts so much more hearing it.

"How did you know?" Charlie asks.

"Know what?" I control my anger and stay with him.

"That I was missing?"

"Your dad came to my house."

The stillness of the church, as it's supposed to be at this hour, takes over the room. "He did?" Charlie sounds like a child.

"Yeah," I say, and because there's no point going into it now I laugh. "It was fine. I mean, hey, we found you, right? He'll be happy."

But Charlie doesn't laugh, and I feel stupid for trying to make light of anything in this moment. He looks at me, bloody, beaten, and just back to consciousness, and yet he says, "It's people like him who created this." He looks down. "Dad's not religious. Never has been. It's not the church; it's the hate."

I'd love to continue this conversation, because I am amazed at his spirit, his clarity, but Tom and his men rush in, followed by a crew of EMTs and I'm pushed back into the shadows, where I remain, and watch them work on Charlie.

When he's upright, moved to a pew and they're checking his vitals, Mr. McCarthy comes in. He sits down next to his son and wraps him up in a hug, His cries echo off the walls and whatever I felt about him is tucked away. Because I understand him more. We're not that different. Both of us are battling with all this anger in spite of the love we feel.

My family arrives moments later, and they sit with me in a pew in the church belonging to the congregation that hates me, led by the man whose daughter loved me, and died for that sin. There are no words.

We watch the EMTs patch up Charlie, who sneaks furtive glances over at us, and his father, who talks to the police. The reporters and their lights and their cameras are outside. It's another show and at the center is someone I love.

Tom breaks away and joins us. He hovers at first and then sits next to Dad.

"So, what now?" I ask.

Tom leans forward, hands clasped between his knees. "I wish he had seen them. I wish we had faces. But we don't."

"Still, it's something, and the paper, it's Matthison's, just like Beth and Mary."

"It is. But look where we are. Matthison has stacks of it in the back room."

I lean across Dad so I don't have to yell. "Are you saying that this is some kind of coincidence? Look where we are." I throw Tom's words back at him.

"I know, Avery. I do. Matthison's in custody. We told him it was for his own protection."

"And Calder?"

"Him too."

I sit back and then slouch into the pew. It doesn't make sense. Not that it ever did. But the fact that there were two shifts my thinking. Whoever it is has a partner. That could explain some of the things at school, how he's aware of what's what. But it doesn't explain the cemetery. It doesn't explain how he seems to be everywhere and yet nowhere all at once.

My phone has been quiet, and I wonder how long it will be until I hear from him. But at the same time I wonder if it even matters. Tom can't trace the number. The killer could be standing outside right now, watching us, and we'd never know. But it's also not about the technology. That's not what matters. It's what Charlie said. The more fundamental communication: hate.

At the center of all this is me, as well as a steaming pile of hatred. No amount of tech savviness or sleuthing police work will be able to explore and understand all the avenues that hate travels. New ones open every day. But so do inroads of compassion and understanding and love. They have to, or we'd be choked off on all the anger. There would be no light.

"Tom, clear this place." My voice is direct, and it perks everyone up.

"What do you mean?" Tom says.

"I want everyone to leave. I have something I need to do."

He starts to argue, but then seems to sense what I'm saying. He stops, looks around and it must click. I'm already here. All I have to do is get down on my knees.

"Okay, Avery. I can give you a few minutes. We have to come back in. We have to process this crime scene."

"I can wait, Tom. It's not as if I want to do this."

He stands. "No, we'll do this now. It's right."

Dad grips me around the shoulders and Mom takes my hand. "You have nothing to repent for, Avery." She then kisses the top of my head.

"This isn't just about me, though. So, for them, for Charlie, for Beth, for Mary, I'll do what he wants."

"If the ends justify the means," Dad says, and then like Mom, kisses me. "I don't like this," he says into my hair, "but I'll be damned if I can think of another way."

They stand and Ty says, "Good luck," and they walk down the aisle.

Tom's making the rounds, and some have already left. He goes to the EMTs and they nod and get Charlie to his feet. He looks at me, curiously, his eyes still bright. I wave and his father joins him, so I turn away and face the front of the church.

The crucifix is enormous, maybe twenty feet tall, and even in the shadows, I can see the droplets of blood rolling down Jesus' side. They say he died for us, for our sins. I wonder if he thinks the sacrifice was worth it.

Tom crouches down next to me. "Okay, Av. You've got five minutes."

I turn and look, and sure enough, the church is empty, except for the two of us. "Okay, thanks," I say, but then feel panicked. "Tom, I don't know how to pray, to do what I'm supposed to."

He grips my shoulder. "Avery, this place may be bugged, the killer may be watching and listening and recording, I have no idea. But I also don't think it matters if you get the words right. You just need to speak from the heart. That's what he wants. Some piece of you. This is a game, and you are the ultimate chip." He pauses, looks me in the eye. "It's not going to be easy, but do what needs to be done."

His footsteps echo down the hall and then the door creaks open and falls shut. I am alone.

I stand up and walk toward the altar, the same place where less than a week ago the reverend gave his eulogy for Mary.

My legs buckle as I kneel on the top step, just outside the sacred area where Reverend Matthison practices. If it's him behind this, and he's recording, I can only imagine the smile that will spread across his face when he watches me. If it's Calder, then at this point, he must also have some in. Maybe with the reverend. Maybe they are the duo, and he'll watch alongside him. Or if it's someone we haven't thought of, maybe he's streaming this to wherever he is. Fuck them all. Because at the end, it's not about any of them. This is for Mary. The death stops with her, where it should have never begun.

I close my eyes and open my mouth and my voice stutters out. "God. I'm here. To repent." I take a deep breath. "In Your eyes I know I have sinned. I know that how You made me, and what I have done to my body is not in Your liking. I know that my pride and ego have made me into something I'm not."

Every word of this lie burns like a candle being snubbed on my tongue. But I continue.

"I am sorry for my actions, and ask for Your forgiveness. Because only through You can I actually see. Please forgive me."

I continue to kneel, long after I've finished, because I'm afraid if I move, if I open my eyes, then the words I've spoken will come to life and I will be judged. But nothing happens. The room is quiet and dark and still just a room. I open my eyes. The altar is the same as when I closed them. The air is as heavy and somber. I am still me, and no amount of words will change that.

I stand and turn toward the door, feeling lighter, but also feeling ashamed. I gave in. I had to, but still, I caved.

The chime echoes like a church bell. I reach for my phone and my hand is already shaking. The illumination seeps across the pews around me and I read in the semidark.

You may never be rewarded in His kingdom, but for now, you may find what you are looking for.

The text bubble writhes at the bottom of my screen and I wait, breathlessly.

See no evil, hear no evil, speak no evil. Words to live by. But they are not complete. There is one last piece, and then the puzzle will be solved.

I don't understand. That's the extent to which I know the saying. How can there be more? Or does he mean . . .

Tom walks through the door and sees me on my phone.

"Avery, what happened?"

"Have you found her heart?"

He looks back and goes to the door, puts his heel against it. "Avery, why are you asking? What did he text you?"

"It's the last piece, he said that. He said it would solve the puzzle."

"We haven't found it, Avery."

I think of the expression, see the stupid monkeys associated with it, but know without understanding how I know, that they are not the source. It's closer, and I hear it reverberating within me: *See no evil, hear no evil, speak no evil, and you shall be pure of heart.* The reverend's own words, spoken as he practiced his sermon. That day, the day that changed everything. He spoke those words as Mary and I slipped out of the house. And through them I know the truth.

CHAPTER 22

We pull onto the gravel driveway of the Matthisons' home and the rocks pop beneath the tires, much like my nerves are striking every part of me. Tom agreed to take me once I told him what we'd find. I'd come to the conclusion on my own, and if I'm right, everything should end where it began.

The house is bright, most of the lights on, cars are still parked in the driveway. A police cruiser sits here as well.

"I thought you said they brought him into custody."

"They were supposed to." Tom slams the car into park. "Do not get out," he says to me and goes inside. A moment later he returns to the driveway, with Officer Wright behind him. Since he left the keys in the ignition, I lower my window and listen.

"How is he still here? You had direct orders to take him in."

"Tom, come on. His church is a crime scene. His daughter's been murdered. Do you really think I needed to bring him in? I told him I'd stay with him. What's the difference?"

Tom pins back his shoulders like he's getting ready to punch the asshole in his face. "The difference is that I can't search his fucking house when he's here!"

Wright holds up his hands. "Whoa, whoa, why are we searching him?"

Tom cocks his head, looks his colleague over. "Why are you even asking? Are you protecting him from something?"

Now Wright gets his back up. "Are you questioning my integrity?"

"Yes. I. Am." With every word, Tom has taken a step closer. He's now in the cop's face.

"How dare you? Just because I worship at his church doesn't mean I can't do my job."

"Bullshit! Or he wouldn't be here. Now I'm giving you one minute to clear him out, or I'm coming in and doing your job for you."

Wright steps back and forth, looking like he's deciding whether to hit Tom or listen to his orders. He spins on his heel and goes inside. Tom walks back to the car and comes to my window. It figures he assumed it would be open.

"Jesus fucking Christ," he says.

"Exactly." I can't offer much more, because I'm still focused on my one goal. Tom knows that I believe I will find it, but I haven't told him what I have to do to retrieve it. Or whether I truly can.

We wait and nothing happens. Neither the reverend nor the asshole cop emerge. Tom shoves the car and heads back up the driveway. This time I pop out and follow him inside.

The Matthisons are sitting in the living room, reading separate Bibles in separate chairs. They squint up at us when we enter. Even I know this is not the air of someone about to be detained. Wright is nowhere around.

"Where is Officer Wright?" Tom asks, but the Matthisons don't answer. They stare at me.

"What is *it* doing here?" the reverend says.

Tom holds up his hands. "Easy, Reverend Matthison. I'm just looking for Officer Wright."

"Then why in the name of all that is holy have you brought this abomination into my home?" He stands as he finishes, flushed red and fuming.

There is no time for this. Something is deeply wrong with this picture. Tom asked the asshole to bring the reverend in, and instead, he seems to have sat with them while they read and prayed. And now he's disappeared.

"Reverend Matthison, please, I don't think you understand. . . ."

I cut Tom off, stepping in front of him and to Matthison. "Go ahead, hit me. Just like you did Mary. Get a belt, a stick, a switch, but make it quick, because the cop who was just here is about to keep you from ever having closure over Mary's death."

Tom grabs my shoulder. "Avery, what?"

"The swimming hole."

I meet the reverend's eyes, so that he feels the understanding of what I've said, and he looks away, ashamed. It's all Tom needs to see before saying to me, "Show me the way."

We charge out the back door and into the night. The woods envelope us as we descend the hill. Up ahead, in the dark, a flashlight is visible, scouring the earth. Tom pulls his gun from his holster.

My lungs burn and my heart hammers, but this is it, there's no time for weakness.

"Put your hands up!" Tom screams and shines his flashlight in Wright's eyes.

He scrambles for his gun and Tom knocks him in the head with his own. Then he stands over him, light still shining in his now bloody eye and wrenches the gun from his holster.

He tosses it aside and then pins the cop with his knee. Tom rolls and then handcuffs him. He sits back once Wright has been cuffed.

"What were you looking for, huh?" Tom yells. "What were you hoping to find? Some last piece of evidence so you could keep playing your game?"

Wright stares straight ahead, and I can tell he won't say a word.

Tom shakes his head and stands, pops his flashlight along the ground where the cop was. I join him, looking at the ground. Nothing's been disturbed. I don't think he knew where to look. But how could that be? How could that be if he's the one responsible?

Two attackers.

I leave Tom and go to Wright. I get down on my knees and I pull out his phone. I pull up his text history and see the message to myself. My brain is overwhelmed, overcome by so many emotions. But I force myself to stay calm. There are too many unanswered questions, and still one piece missing.

"Who else did this?"

He acts as if I'm not there.

"Two of you attacked Charlie. So you, and some

other whacked out holy roller did this. You might as well tell me before Tom works you over."

His eyes widen, but he still doesn't speak.

"You know as well as I do, that the Lord forgives, so long as you ask for it. But that doesn't mean I have to." I grab his balls and twist. "She loved me, you know. Mary and I loved each other." I twist again. "And this stupid faith or hate or whatever you call it took that away from us." Now I yank. "And then you took her, period." I twist again and he cries out.

"Avery, what are you doing?"

I ignore my uncle. "How did you know to come here? Who did this with you?" I lean in, my lips brushing over his ear. "If you don't tell me, I'll rip your fucking dick off. You know I still need one of my own."

"She didn't tell me!" he screams. "She didn't tell me."

I go to twist for more, but Tom puts his hand on me. "No. That's enough."

I shrug him off. "I'll decide that."

Tom grabs my wrist. "Avery, you do this and you're no better than him."

His words infuriate me, his tone boils me inside, and the truth undoes me. "I loved her, you fucking asshole! And you killed her!"

"That's why we killed her! Because she loved you back!" Wright screams and Tom shines his flashlight over his face. "You filthy animal. You don't deserve anything, not love, not pity, not respect. *You* deserved to die, but Mary always protected you. Always! She couldn't even understand how she was denouncing her own religion to save you from the wrath you deserve." He catches his breath but then continues. "So she had to be stopped, so that we could stop all of you."

I am stunned silent. My anger has faded. My heart has stopped racing. The truth is out, and I am to blame.

"Avery?" Tom crouches down next to me.

I don't answer. I'm not sure if I can even speak.

"Avery, stay with me. Remember why we're here."

I remember, but it feels as if it doesn't matter anymore. It won't change anything. He's admitted what he's done. Tom will find out who his sidekick is. So why am I not elated? Why aren't I thrilled that we've figured it out, that we've won?

I hear footsteps and look up and see the Matthisons.

The reverend opens his mouth to speak, but Mrs. Matthison tugs on his arm and he shuts it. Tom moves away from me and to them.

"I'm sure you're confused. I'll explain what I can," Tom says.

"Why did you come here? What's going on?" Matthison asks.

"There is still evidence, and I believe it is on your property."

"*You* believe, or *It* does?"

The words stings. Such a little thing, but now, in this moment, the last thing I need is more ridicule.

Tom clears his throat. "You're upset, I understand. But now is not the time for that. Avery is here to help. Did you hear what Office Wright confessed?"

"I did," Matthison says, and I'm surprised at the strength of his voice.

"So you understand the situation. He and someone else murdered your daughter."

Mrs. Matthison breaks into sobs. They tear through me, sounding so much like Mary's.

"I understand, Officer Chase. At least I think I do. But I don't know what to say. I don't know what you expect from me right now. I . . . can't . . ." He falters and his own tears fall.

As stunned as I was, I am completely undone now. The world is upside down.

"You don't have to say anything." Tom's voice is gentle over the Matthisons' pain.

"But I do," I say, before I even realize I'm speaking. Tom's eyes flash a warning, but he clearly doesn't understand I'm not looking for a fight.

I walk over to the Matthisons and I take a deep breath. "You know how much Mary meant to me, and I believe you understand, maybe even more so now, how much I meant to her."

"Oh, I do," Matthison says. "Enough that she died for you."

"No!" I scream, because I refuse to let him do that. "She was murdered because of who she was. There's a difference. She was better than him," I say, pointing to Wright. "She was filled with more love than you ever have been or ever will be."

"Avery!" Tom barks.

I ignore him. I deserve this moment. Mary does, even more. "And because of that, I want to help you. I want to find what has been left, so you can know all of her is home. But I need you to answer one question."

Matthison turns from me, unwilling to look me in the eyes. "One. What is it?"

"Who did you tell about that day in the swimming hole?"

His head snaps around. "Why does that matter? She made one mistake. You would have let her keep sinning if I hadn't caught you."

"None of that matters now," I say. "But your answer does. Who did you tell?"

Matthison's eyes light up, and in them I see the flame of his hatred burn so bright. But I refuse to look away. I am before him. He sees me. There's no hiding anything.

"The entire congregation. I made her tell the story. I made her repent her sins in front of everyone, so that none of the rest would ever be tempted."

As he speaks I can see it. Mary in the front of the church, where I was just kneeling, asking for my own forgiveness. How could someone do that to his own daughter? What good could he possibly have imagined it would do?

The answer lies handcuffed behind us. It killed her. But I won't say that, I won't pour salt in the wound. Nothing good will ever come of that. I'm here because of Mary, and for her, I will do what I have promised.

I leave them and climb into the water, and it cinches up my breath like a drawstring. I breathe through my nose and calm myself. "Give me your flashlight, Tom."

He hands it over. "This is waterproof, right?"

Tom nods, and I see in his face the revelation of where this is going.

I pop on the flashlight and lose all of them to the singular spot in the water. I go under, the water clawing at my head in its brilliant cold. But I ignore it. I shine the light along the bottom, I look for disruption, and then I see. I go up for air and then quickly return. I begin digging.

It takes a number of trips, but I unearth the lid, and then the upper portion of the jar. I take one last steeling breath and go under. The jar comes loose in my hand, and I bring it to the surface.

The human heart is unmistakable. Even pulled from a body, the sea creature–like appearance of the aorta and pulmonary veins remain. Mary's fills the entirety of the jar. And unlike the other pieces, this one—I'll bet like all the rest when they were still in the jar—is labeled with her name, her age and

ERIC DEVINE

255

gender, along with the date the jar was sealed—the day she disappeared.

There is a piece of paper sealed in plastic, bound to the side. I shine the flashlight over and read:

> The preparations of the heart in man, and the answer of the tongue, is from the LORD.
>
> All the ways of a man are clean in his own eyes; but the LORD weigheth the spirits.
>
> Commit thy works unto the LORD, and thy thoughts shall be established.
>
> The LORD hath made all things for himself: yea, even the wicked for the day of evil.
>
> Every one that is proud in heart is an abomination to the LORD; though hand join in hand, he shall not be unpunished.

If I could shiver any more than I already am, I would. Here is the answer, written in words straight from the Bible. I climb out of the water and as much as I can see Tom wants the jar, he also seems to understand where it must go first.

I hand it to Matthison, who looks dumbstruck. He refuses to look at what is in his hands.

"Read it." I shine the light. Tom steps behind the reverend so he can see.

Matthison's face closes on itself, and I can't tell if it's fury or sorrow.

"Her heart wasn't pure," Wright says. We look at him. "It's like you said, reverend, the analogy of the flock you use, and how nature kills the weakest."

Matthison looks confused. "Nature. Yes. The Lord. Not us."

"But we are Him."

Matthison shakes and almost drops the jar. But he regains his grasp and holds it up. "This is not the work of the Lord. Neither are you."

Officer Wright laughs. "Only He can judge me."

"Don't worry, He will," Matthison says.

Sirens are blazing around us, and in the distance red and blue lights and heading our way. Tom must have called this in while I was underwater. Good. We have all of the evidence.

"I think you three should head inside, if that's okay with you, Avery. I'll stay here with him."

I'm too cold to argue. I'll just stand at the doorway until someone picks me up, either my parents or Officer Howard. "No problem," I say and head toward the house. The Matthisons fall in behind me, and it is such a surreal scene. I know I should feel more than the numbness I do. But I understand that in time I will. And that's okay for now.

"I don't know how this can be true," Mrs. Matthison says to her husband. "One of our own. And . . ." She stops talking and I turn to listen. "He was so close with the youth group. How could he? Mary . . . Lord my poor Mary. And his niece was so close to her." She breaks into sobs and the reverend holds her.

I feel horrible eavesdropping on Mary's parents, especially in this moment. It's like I'm a child again, but what I'm hearing is infinitely worse, and so I must speak.

"Who is his niece?"

Only the reverend looks at me. His wife continues to cry on his shoulder, and I'm sure, in a moment, will be inconsolable as this truth is fully realized. And so I only have a moment in which to get this answer. And I know this answer is important because of what the reverend did, marching Mary in front of everyone, like some modern day witch. They all knew about us and that day in the swimming hole, including the youth group, the ones who it seems Officer Wright was close with. Or at least his niece.

I step closer. "Please, Reverend. I know you are smart enough to understand that Wright wasn't alone in this. His hatred spread to others, and one of them was his accomplice." He doesn't speak but holds me in a steady and unwavering gaze. I step closer. "Before someone tips her off and she runs and hides and then you have to wait for justice, tell me. I will get the justice Mary deserves."

"Why should I trust you?" His voice is piercing, in spite of everything else.

"You never have. And so maybe now you realize that was your mistake all along." I'm writhing with anger, am shivering from the cold, and have a heart that is turning to sludge, and yet, I'm composed in front of him. Have to be. This is how Mary always stood before him.

He looks away and his face is caught in the blue and red light of the approaching cruisers. "Can you find out why? Beyond what Wright said. Do you think you can get an answer for why they murdered my daughter?"

When he turns and looks at me, I know there is no acceptable answer besides yes. Even though I'm not sure I can, I agree. "For once, you and I have the exact same interest."

The reverend nods at this and then kisses the top of his wife's head. "Eva Clemson."

CHAPTER 23

I stick close to the house as the officers descend upon it. The reverend moved his wife inside, and I'm sure they will focus their attention on her, first.

The cops find Tom and start taping off the scene under his direction. The energy is high. These cops seem relieved to have their suspect, even if it is one of their own. Which means I have a short window of time to do what I intend to. They'll be looking for me; they'll be talking to the Matthisons; someone will figure out what I have, that they need to get to Eva.

I slink to Tom's cruiser, undetected, and hop behind the wheel. His computer is open, running whatever system it is they have. I pull up a box with a series of tabs for Name, Address history, Aliases, Photos. I click the name tab and type *Eva Clemson* into the right fields, and a few names pop up, but only one is seventeen.

Water drips from my nose onto the keyboard. I ignore it and mouse over the address. It's hyper-linked. I look back at the crime scene. Tom, after having his men cordon off every inch possible, is now retracing our footsteps from the back door. I watch him secure the tape to the house, and then turn his back to me. He starts walking and I click the address.

The GPS system comes on, with the highlighted route glowing bright. She's five minutes away, her family farm just over the hill.

My hands feel heavy in my lap, and when I look down, it's as if I'm holding Mary's heart again. How could anyone do this, even if it is in the name of their faith? Why would they be so brutal?

The engine roars to life and the lights pop on. The crime scene is illuminated in the distance. With all the activity, no one is paying attention to a cruiser rolling down the driveway; there's too much commotion.

I drive and try to formulate a plan, as well as what I'll say to her, how I'll get a confession. She's going to know something is up, and if she figures it out, I'm in serious danger. All the work on her farm, rendering animals for sale, for meals. All her brute strength. That strength she turned on Mary. I say one last prayer and take the turn up the hill.

Eva's house sits to the side of a series of barns that are the entryway to fields of corn and hay and alfalfa, and pens for pigs and chickens and horses and cows. I kill the lights and park the car behind a tree off to the side of the property. I keep my eyes peeled as I walk up to the front door.

The doorbell echoes through the house, and I realize I have no idea what time it is. They're farmers, and are most likely asleep.

But a moment later, Eva's father peers through the window, worn out looking but not in his pajamas. He can't seem to place me, and the porch light pops on overhead. He opens the door, but stands within it. "Can I help you?"

I'm dripping wet, and can only imagine how pathetic I look to this burly man. "Is Eva home?"

He takes a step closer. "And why would you want to know?"

I can't judge his tone, it's so utterly flat. Does he recognize me or not? "Just a friend. Had some car trouble and fell in the pond back aways."

He looks over me. "Car trouble? I don't see a car."

"That's the trouble. It ran out of gas, I think, it's a mile or so back. I'm freezing and just want to get warm. Your house was closest. Please let me inside and then I'll call my parents. Cell's dead. I'm sorry to bother you."

He draws a deep grunt from his throat. Then his hand is on my shoulder. "It's no problem, son. We can help. Jeremiah's clothes should fit you. What's your name?"

"Av . . ." I stop myself. I am in the lion's den. There's no doubt he'll put two and two together. "Avett."

His hand loosens. "Huh, I don't think we've met, Avett."

I put out my hand.

"Right, nice to meet you, Avett," Mr. Clemson says. "Let's get you dried off and then you can call your parents. If you want to say hi to Eva, she's at the top of the stairs."

He walks into the house, leaving me alone, and once he's far enough away, I spring.

I head up the stairs. The wall on the right side is covered with family photos and pictures of Eva and her brothers at the county fair, hunting with their father, and on the stand with their medals. I shudder at the picture of Eva with a knife, eyes not seeing the camera as she debones a fish, her uncle just over her shoulder.

All the doors are closed, so I knock on the one directly at the top, hoping her father was being direct.

The bed squeaks and the door opens, and the killer stands framed by the lamplight behind her.

She doesn't speak. Eva takes me in, looking at the sopping wet mess that I am. "Avery," she says, "what are you doing here?"

I resist saying what I want to say, unleashing on her as I've been imagining. Instead, I push my hair back and lean against her doorframe. "Car trouble. You wouldn't believe. I remembered that you lived out here and your dad's getting me your brother's clothes." I roll my eyes.

"Daddy saw you. What did he say?"

"Well, I didn't tell him my name. Sorry, I didn't want him to throw me out. He said I'd fit into Jeremiah's stuff."

She looks me over, a little too shocked, I think, seeing me here.

"But, here's the thing," I say and stand straight again. "I don't know if it was the other day at school, or everything that has happened, but now that I'm here with you, I'm thinking that wearing Jeremiah's clothes isn't what I want."

Eva's eyes grow exponentially. The cross at her neck flutters. "Avery, what are you saying?"

I grab her hands like she has done to me so many times, like the flock does to one another. "Eva, it's time for my redemption." The tears that flood my eyes are real, because what I've said is so painful. But I'm running this marathon to the very last mile.

"You don't mean, you can't possibly . . ." She doesn't finish. Eva squeezes tight and crosses herself.

"There you are. Here, I've got the clothes."

Mr. Clemson's words make my legs weak.

Eva moves around me though, to her father. "Daddy, you're embarrassing her."

I feel his confusion in the way he says, "Uh."

"She doesn't need Jeremiah's stuff. I'll give her mine."

"But I thought," he says, "I thought she was . . ."

"Never mind what you thought and quit making her uncomfortable. She's been through enough tonight. I'm going to get her set up, and then we'll take care of her car."

I absorb every *her* and *she* and do not wince. Now's not the time for my pain.

Eva comes back to me, grabs my hand, pulls me into her room, and shuts the door. "Men," she throws up her hands, "so dumb."

I'm momentarily paralyzed. Her room is just like the wall, adorned in so many ways with her vast accomplishments with her farm animals. She sees me looking. "Lot of blood, sweat, and tears right there."

"Right," I say, but the realizations I'm coming to have nothing to do with her farmer girl ways.

"Avery, I cannot tell you how long I have waited for this moment." She goes to her closet then turns back to me. "I've prayed for years. *He* listens." She turns back into her closet, and I'm at a loss. I knew I needed to get here, to be here before Tom and the cops, but what now?

"Peel off those clothes, sweetie. Just us girls, no shame in that."

And her words pull me back to what I've said, what I've implied, and now what must be done, for the reverend and especially for Mary.

I get off my shoes and socks and then peel my jeans and let them slump to the floor. I hesitate to go further.

Eva tosses an armful of clothes onto the bed. "Oh, look at you. I'll help you out of that sweatshirt. Bend over."

I do and thrust my arms forward. She grabs the sleeves and off comes my shirt and sweatshirt. I stand in only my binder and underwear.

"Well, I've always wondered how you kept them so flat." Eva eyes my binder with fascination. "Now how are we going to get that off? Seems tighter than a tarp." She scowls and before I can answer she turns to a drawer. "Here." She holds up a long knife with a curved tip and a serrated bottom.

This is what Mary must have seen. I draw on this and I find strength.

But then Eva's at my back and the tip of the blade touches my skin. "Don't worry, I won't cut you."

I close my eyes and pray. I speak to Mary directly, asking her to watch over me, because for all I know this entire family could be a bunch of psychos and will bury my body or feed it to the pigs before any officer comes out here.

The blade draws up and in a smooth line and breaks the tension of the binder from my body. I don't feel any pain or blood pooling into my lower back.

"There we go," Eva says and steps in front of me. She reaches around and grabs the now two sides of the binder and tugs. It comes away from my body like a broken suit of armor, and I stand before this monster, naked from the waist up.

Her breath catches and she lets the binder fall while cupping her hands over her mouth. I wait for the laughter to peal. Instead, she cries.

"Oh, Avery, you are so beautiful. I never would have imagined." She pauses, dries her eyes. "This must have been what Mary saw in you." The last statement ignites my insides. It burns in a white-hot flash, but I have to contain it. It's not time, not yet. I have to keep playing with fire.

"It's tough to tell what anyone ever sees," I say.

Eva's face is open to me. "That is so true, Avery. But if we keep our eyes toward the Lord, He will guide us."

I nod, because I can't respond to that.

Eva turns and tosses through her clothes. "Here, I'll turn while you put these on." She holds a pair of panties out to me. It takes all the strength I have to take them from her.

I slide off my soaked boxer briefs and then step into the dry and ill-fitting panties. She hands over a pair of black leggings and a bright pink long-sleeve shirt. "Sorry I can't give you a bra. Your chest is larger than mine." She laughs at this and I smile along.

But once I'm dressed my smile disappears. I am done with her game of dress-up. It's time to move in on her.

"Sit, sit, let me brush your hair."

I sit before her vanity and spot the knife on her nightstand, as well as my torn binder on the floor. My heart sinks impossibly deeper.

Eva works the brush through, "Those pigtails the other day were awful, but at least you've kept it long enough to work with. I can style this." She puts her hands on my shoulders. "What did it for you, Avery? What brought you to me?"

It feels like a door has opened. I step through. "I was at the Matthisons'." Her grip on my shoulders tightens.

"Really? Why?"

It's disorienting looking up at her in the mirror. "I had some things to clear up. There's always been some bad blood with the family, and now that they've captured Mary's killer, I wanted . . ."

"What?" she screams. Eva must realize how loud she was, because she sits on the corner of her bed. "I mean, how do you know?"

I turn to her now. "You know I've been involved because of the killer reaching out to me." She nods. "Well, that also means Tom's been keeping me in the loop when I have something new. Tonight, he brought me out to the Matthisons' and, well," I pause, hoping to make this sound dramatic enough, "he had to confront your uncle. He all but admitted what he'd done."

"Randall? What? I can't believe it."

I sit back. "I didn't tell you which uncle." Along with the showcase of farmhand talent, the Clemsons' wall is also filled with family pictures. Very large ones.

She turns away. "It only made sense, since you were talking about Tom and he's on the force with him. But still." She doesn't finish.

"So it makes sense to you that a cop would kill someone?"

Eva plays with the brush. "No. No, it's more than that." She looks up at me. "Is that why you really came? To rub this in my face? To make me feel sorry for you?"

I put up my hands. "No, not at all. I told you I wanted to repent. I think I got into the accident once I understood what had happened, and as I thought about everything, I asked myself what Mary would want from me now. I think she led me here."

Eva smiles, but it's the practiced one she puts on for us at school, not the genuine one that exists post-killing, forever imprinted on the pictures along the stairs.

"Why would she want you here?"

"With you, of course. She told me all about you. Back when we were friends. I doubt much changed with the two of you, though."

Eva leans in, clearly in love with her story. "What? What did she say about me?"

"How kind you are, how smart, how beautiful?"

Eva smiles. "Anything else?"

I look up, as if searching for the word. "How righteous. Even though she was the reverend's daughter, she felt that she had a lot to learn from you."

Even in the dim light I can see her blush.

"She said that?"

"Yeah. That you had a *piety* that most don't." I look her in the eye. "Is that something you learned from your uncle?"

She starts to smile but then asks, "What do you mean by that?"

"Well, he was involved with the youth group, right?"

"Yeah. So?"

"He said that Mary was murdered because she didn't want to denounce me, that she was going against her faith by not proclaiming that I was a sinner. If that's what he believed, I'm guessing he taught you the same."

"Well, you were a sinner, but look at you now." She holds up her hands in a beauty pageant way, but it looks and feels so false.

"Look at me now. Sitting across from the girl who helped killed Mary."

The room goes deathly still. Eva's face is barely visible, but the red and blue lights bouncing through the window behind her are. Time's running out.

"I don't know what you're talking about, and I think you should go."

"Tell me why," I say.

"Daddy!" she yells. "Help!"

I clamp my hands over her mouth. "I know the reverend used Mary as an example. Is that why you did it? Is it because in spite of him telling her to repent, you knew she wasn't being honest, that she still had feelings for me?"

I let go of her mouth, fully prepared to punch her in the face if she tries to scream again.

"Doing God's work is, and always will be, difficult. But just because it's difficult doesn't mean it shouldn't be undertaken. You've taken the easy way out, going with your feelings, never stopping to question how what you chose affects everyone else."

"Is that what you do? You spend time considering all of your hatred and how it hurts? Is that God's work?"

The tendons in Eva's neck pop as she struggles with this moment, with her words. "Mary was the same way. It didn't matter how many times the reverend reprimanded her, she always thought with only her heart. The teachings, the scripture, none of it mattered. Just like with Calder. She made him have sex. And then he went to the reverend, told him what had happened, that he didn't want to anymore. And when her father confronted her, she all but spit on the Bible and stormed out of the house."

I'm having trouble staying in this moment and doing what I've come to do, because if even parts of her story are true, my heart breaks all over for Mary. No one in her life had any tolerance for who she was and what she desired. The splashing lights draw me back.

"Were you there? You watched this fight?"

Eva nods. "Yes! That's how we learn. My uncle wanted me to help lead the youth group. Mary was the biggest challenge. And so he was the first person the reverend called when Calder came to him. And he brought me to the house so we could all witness her antics."

"What did she do, Eva? What was so wrong in your eyes? Having sex with Calder?"

"No!" Eva moves closer to me, her eyes wild, and I am very aware of how much force there is behind her. "It wasn't that they'd had sex. So long as she asked for forgiveness, she would have been granted it. It's that when her father brought it up, she turned on him. She told him this was just like with you, Avery. That he'd acted in the same way when he found the two of you, and that she had hated him ever since that day because he drove you away." She pauses, and seems to savor how destroyed I must look. "That's how we knew there was no saving her. Unrepentant. Sex-driven. And protector of freaks like you."

Somehow I find my voice. "The weakest of the flock."

Eva's eyes go rapturously wide. "Exactly!"

"You must kill them to save the others." The words feel like poison coming out of my mouth.

Eva clasps my hand. "You do understand, Avery. Oh, He is good, for you see what even Mary couldn't."

"So how? How did you? I just can't understand that. Help me see." I've heard enough, but I also know if I can play her game, I'll hear it all. And as much as my heart can't take any more, I know it has to. I need the truth.

"How? It was easy. No different than wrastlin' a pig. She took off and we told the reverend to let her walk it off. Then we pretended to go home and found her walking not far from here. Near the pond. Scooped her up, easy peasy. Randall's been working on the farm since he was a boy."

I stare, because it's all I can do.

"We took her to the barn. And the rest, well, I'm good at cutting. All those parts, Randall knew how to preserve them and what he was going to do with them. That they'd drive the reverend, your uncle, and hopefully you, insane." She smiles. "He knew to move the body in the rain, to cover our tracks. 'Reverse police work' he called it. And the notes were his idea, too. Perfect, I think. A shepherd who cannot keep his own sheep should not have a flock. It's time for Matthison to go. It's a new day, and we can't let our faith produce freak-loving girls like Mary."

"But the reverend, he hates me."

"True. But deeds, not words, that's what this world needs."

My head lists, but the lights keep playing across the walls and floor. I think Eva has been so caught up in her story that she hasn't seen them. But as soon as she does, I'm as good as dead if I don't keep her talking.

"I still don't understand. Killing Mary and then carving her up. Who did that help? Who have you saved?"

She looks over her shoulder and squints at the lights. There are footsteps on the stairs. She hears them. And I hope they belong to help. Because as much as I know I shouldn't, I have to. I have to speak.

"He is good, Eva. I prayed tonight and He brought me here, to you. And now you've confessed. My uncle, the freak-loving man he is, can arrest you, and you and your monster of an uncle can pay for what you did. I am as unrepentant as Mary, you fucking bitch!"

I am so close to Eva, I can see the contortion of her face, the tiny twitches that display her absolute disgust with me. In one elegant move, she puts all her self-righteousness into action.

The blade feels hot, not at all what I would expect from a knife thrust into my chest. I cough and blood splatters across Eva's face. She smiles and pats my cheek.

"This was always about you, Avery. I would have killed you first had Mary not disgusted me more. You have no faith and you're going to burn in hell, along with Mary." She stares down at me, her eyes again wild, her mouth drawing into a sneer. "And if I had time, I'd cut off little pieces of you and send them to your family. I'd bottle them in my uncle's jars, just like those specimens you love. You're a freak that should be labeled and preserved as a reminder. That's what this town needed, what you needed, a reminder. The Lord giveth and the Lord taketh away. Never abuse the gift of life He created for you."

Eva grabs the handle of the knife, and I know she's going to pull it out, because she knows as well as I do, that's how you kill. It's not the wounded heart that ends life, but how it spills forth once past mending.

But I've known this forever, and as much as the pain threatens to make me pass out, I grip the hilt with as much strength I have left. She pulls against me, but then a hand touches her shoulder. She wheels around and I stagger back.

Officers swoop in and handcuff Eva as quickly as Tom did her uncle. My vision starts to recede, but I force myself to stay awake, to see this through.

Someone's calling for an ambulance and they're propping Eva upright and hauling her away. "I'm innocent! She's the monster!"

As I pass out, I wonder if she's referring to me, or to Mary. It brings me comfort to know that she is truly speaking about herself.

CHAPTER 24

The monitor beats a steady rhythm, much like the rain after Mary died. I stare at the machine, the fact that I'm still alive, and yet I can still feel that rain, that hope. I've been in the hospital for seven days, and I feel no better than when I came out of the coma.

Eva almost succeeded. She came within fractions of killing me. Had she pulled that knife, I never would have left her room. But I did, with a punctured lung, a torn aorta, and a shit-ton of blood loss. They put me in a drug-induced coma for two days, just to keep me safe.

From what they tell me, the town prayed. People said kind things about me on television. For a moment, I was more than just parts and confusion. Apparently, I mattered. But I saw none of this, and I'm glad I didn't. This wasn't about me.

I still want Mary back.

When I do come around, after days of dreams that felt uncomfortably real, I remember all over again that Mary is dead. I want to go back to Eva's room and I want to pull that knife out.

Because now I have to live with this.

Mom held me tight and expected tears. Dad brought homemade pudding and thought I'd be elated. Tyler understood. He sat on the bed with me and we watched stupid movies and didn't talk. It's exactly what I needed, because I'm hollowed out, devoid of emotion. It's worse than the lowest levels of depression I've endured. Maybe it's the guilt, or just the letdown from the intensity. It's impossible to know and all my psychiatrist can say is "Give it time." That and up my meds.

But partly I understand this zombie state I'm in. When it was an investigation, when my mind was trying to solve the problem, put the puzzle back together, I didn't have time to think of anything else. Like the aftermath of knowing. Like the psychological torture. It's worse than I ever imagined. And now the only thing left to put back together is me. But who am I? Can I finally just be Avery Chase?

Beth and Charlie came and saw me, too. It was useless. All of us are still healing in our own ways, and we really didn't know what to say or how to act. Charlie sat in the chair and tried to get me to laugh. Beth stroked my arm. But I stared at the TV like they weren't even there. I just couldn't engage. It's not like we can just move past this. They left me. And I don't blame them. But then they were attacked because of me, because of all that stupid hatred. They still mean the world to me, but I can't figure out how to start over.

And beyond the two of them, I will never see Mary again. I should have understood that before, but I didn't. I sure as hell do now. And so much of my pain comes from not having the closure I need. I never got to say good-bye. I never got to thank her properly, either. I'm alive because of her.

A nurse pops into my room, checks my chart, my vitals, and then smiles. "So you're getting discharged today, how excited are you?"

I adore these nurses, but her perkiness irks me. "Woo."

She swats my arm. "Don't worry, we'll miss you."

I slide down in the bed, my chest throbbing incessantly. "It's like forty degrees out. It's going to kill me. So I'll be back soon."

The nurse puts her hands on her hips. "Well, I doubt that's likely if a six-inch blade to the chest couldn't."

I don't argue, but I'm also not sure she understands that part of me *wants* to come back. Better if I never have to leave.

A couple of hours later, I'm up and dressed. Still no binder because of the wound, but they agreed to make my daily wrap encompass my entire chest, so it's almost the same. "Where are my parents?" I ask. If they've gone through all of this trouble to get me ready and I have to sit here for hours while they get the paperwork together, I'm going to lose it.

"Outside. They've got a surprise for you." The nurse tilts her head and is incredibly adorable when she does so, but I couldn't care less.

"Really?"

"That's what they tell me. Come on."

I shuffle out with the help of my nurse and to a wheelchair at the entrance. "No."

"You show me you can walk ten feet without it."

I sit down and she wheels me outside.

Forty feels like negative ten. I hunch my coat around my neck and look for my parent's car. Just cabs. Then I see the cruiser. My chest feels like it's been opened back up. Tom has not been in to see me. Dad says he's been so busy trying to wrap up the case, but I know it's more than that. I compromised it all, stole his car, and then almost got killed.

Yet, he gets out of the cruiser and opens the door for me. The nurse and he help me into shotgun. "Thanks," he says to her.

"Get well, Avery. I don't want to see you anytime soon." She winks as she closes the door behind me.

Tom drives but doesn't speak, and I feel sweat break out at my armpits. Two can play at this game. I sit, enjoying the heat and change of scenery and let the silence cover me.

When he pulls off the road, I look around, start to notice the surroundings. I don't like what I see.

We pull up to the Matthisons' and Tom parks the car, kills the ignition.

"No way," I say. "I am not going in there. I don't care that he helped me."

"Avery, listen, please. You owe me that much." Tom's voice is deeper than I remember. He sounds like he's been smoking my cigars. I sit up, and I hate that he is the surprise.

"Okay. I'm listening."

"This isn't for me. This isn't for you. This is for them."

"What more do I owe the Matthisons?"

"Nothing. They just want to see you. I think they want to say thank you properly."

I start to balk, to make excuses, but Tom stops that by saying, "If not for them, for Mary."

I want to tell him that was a cheap shot, real dirty play, but I don't. I stay quiet and wait for him to come help me shuffle in. The sooner we get this over, the better. He gets me under my good side and when we get to the door Mrs. Matthison is already there, holding it open. "Hello, Avery," she says, and it's impossible to deny how much her eyes look like Mary's. And in that recognition, I remember their pain, the way they were tortured. It makes having a seat in their living room a little more palatable.

Tom helps me get situated and then helps Mrs. Matthison get drinks. There are cookies on the coffee table, but what I want to know is where the reverend is.

He walks in, very disheveled, and blinks when he sees me. For a moment I think this is a surprise for him, too, but then he says, "Avery," and sits in the chair across from me.

It's beyond surreal. But my life is clearly a surreal pattern, so why not this?

Mrs. Matthison and Tom return with drinks and then take a seat as well. Then there is quiet. The reverend clears his throat. "Avery, first I want to thank you for all that you did. We've had the opportunity to process your actions, now that we know the full story, and we are simply stunned."

I look at Mary's parents and say nothing. He said *first*, which means there's got to be a second.

"Further," he continues, and then takes a sip of his drink. "Further, *I* would like to apologize." The reverend holds my look when he says this.

I look away and don't know what to do, what to say.

"Avery, I can imagine those words come as a great shock to you, and I must admit they come as a great surprise for me to say. But there they are. I apologize for the way I treated you."

"Why?" I turn and ask. "Why? Because of what I did or because you were wrong?"

"Easy, Av," Tom says.

"No. No, I won't take it easy." I look back at the reverend. "You brought me here, and now you want to throw yourself a little congratulatory party because you've forgiven yourself for being awful, and now you want me to be a part of that?" I lean forward. "No, I won't do that. Mary would hate that this is what you are doing. Remember her last words to you."

This brings tears to Mrs. Matthison's eyes and a stiffened spine to the reverend. Tom looks at me and then shakes his head. I agree. This was a mistake.

"Come on, Tom. I'm done here."

Tom moves, but Mrs. Matthison yells, "Stop!" We all do. "Why do you have to be such a stubborn man, Andrew? *I* know how you feel. We've prayed about this. Why can't you just say what's in your heart?" She stands and knocks over her water and doesn't even glance at it. "Haven't you learned anything? Your actions forced Mary from us. Your own people killed her. Not this boy. He loved her. What's so hard to understand?"

Her words ring and I am dumbstruck that the reverend's not stood up and knocked his wife to the ground. That's how he would have treated Mary.

Instead, he hangs his head.

"It's my fault," he says, his voice as soft as Mary's used to be. "I will admit my mistakes. I am to blame for so much of this." He looks up. "Avery, I am trying. I am trying to understand what my daughter saw in you, how she was able to look past and understand the person within. And why. Why she would bother. Why she would protect you. That is not easy for me. But I promise you, in Mary's name, I am trying."

I say nothing. What he has said is amazing, but I'm not ready to let him off the hook.

"She loved you. I know that. She told me." He's crying now and I'm hanging on by the thinnest will. "That day, after I chased both of you, she said so. And every day after when I tried to beat a different answer out of her." Reverend Matthison buries his face in his hands. "I was wrong," echoes up from his palms. "Not about what the church says. I still believe in the teachings of the Lord, so I still haven't come to terms with who you are. But I know I was wrong to force Mary to admit that her love was wrong. I realize that message. Truth in the Lord is what we seek, and Mary prayed and prayed for me to see it. I have."

I stare at my lap, exhausted by what the reverend confessed, what my life, what Mary's life could have been had he come to this conclusion earlier. But there's no point dwelling there. Somehow we have to move on.

I lean forward, in spite of the pain. I want him to hear me. "Listen to your heart, then. Don't believe only what you see, but what you feel as well. From what I understand, God has always wanted us to love one another. You say you're still searching for your answer, but I think you've found it. Teach about love. Focus on that. Honor Mary."

He reaches out to me, the man who caused all of this, who hated me and who hated his daughter's love of me. But it wasn't just him. It was his followers who took it too far. Eva and her uncle, who believed they were righteous because they were doing God's work. And I think the reverend understands how wrong this notion is. How what they were truly following was their insanity. No religion, no belief system, gives you a pass to kill.

I look at his hand outstretched to me, like I am one of the flock, like I am worthy, finally. He's right and he's wrong, but compassion should always win.

I shake the reverend's hand, and I feel a sense of relief, of having achieved something, not only for Mary but for myself.

We sit and they ask about my hospital stay and we eat cookies. A half hour later and I'm spent. The

Matthisons walk us out, and when we're back in Tom's car, he says, "Thank you."

"Yeah, you're welcome. But can you take me home now? I want my bed."

"Sure, bud. But let me show you one more thing."

Again, I don't resist and he drives. I stare out the window, completely zoned out, until he parks. I sit up and wince at the pain. We're in the cemetery.

"The town made it happen. Gathered the funds to rush order it. They installed it this morning."

I climb out of the car and walk on my own to Mary's angel. It's as beautiful as I imagined, possibly even more so. I touch its wing and the cold stone bites against my hand, but I keep it there until it warms.

"How do you do it, Tom? How do you move on?"

He walks over to me and takes in the angel. "After all this? Damned if I know." He sighs, a big gust that feels like he's releasing tension for us both. "Do the same thing you asked of the reverend."

"What do you mean?"

"Honor Mary. Keep her in your heart, but move on. You have a lot of life ahead of you, Av."

The tears finally fall. I don't bother to wipe them away. "And I owe it to her."

"You do. And to your family, and to your friends, to everyone who cares about you." Tom rubs his face. "I've seen too much death and pain on the job. But I accepted that even before I saw it, back when I put on the badge."

"So I just accept it? It's part of life?"

"To a degree. Doesn't mean you have to like it. And it sure as hell doesn't mean you don't get to do anything about it. But you already know this, Av. You always have."

He's right. Mary knew this, too. Accepted this and did the best she could. She was searching for something that those around her wouldn't let her find. I'm lucky to have witnessed that. Fortunate to have others who are not so encumbered.

"But this case, Tom. It changes things, right?"

He grips my shoulder like he always does. "It does, Avery. There's so much to talk about. All the things you've managed to reveal by demanding people to see the truth. I'm beyond proud of you, bud. But more importantly, you should be proud of yourself. I know you're struggling. Only someone without a heart wouldn't feel what you are. And I think you may have the biggest heart of anyone I know."

Tom's words swirl around me, like the snow that I know will soon fall. The snow that will cover this landscape, blanketing it into beauty, a release from all the darkness.

I let go of the angel's wing and I look up. The statue smiles down on me, and I smile back. I see my past in a moment, in a rush of water, in a swirl of fear, in a search for an answer. And then I look beyond. I look past what I cannot see, into a future that awaits. A place where hopefully I'll find, more than I will search.